PART I

THE CROFTER'S DAUGHTER
VICTORIAN ROMANCE

CATHARINE DOBBS

Copyright © 2023 by Catharine Dobbs

All rights reserved.

No part of this book may be reproduced in any form or by any electronic or mechanical means, including information storage and retrieval systems, without written permission from the author, except for the use of brief quotations in a book review.

PROLOGUE

"I'll never forget ye, Father," she vowed as she closed her eyes...

Winter 1848

The rain was driving against the windows of the croft, and Hannah McGinn looked up from her place by the fire, anxiously awaiting her father's return. Her mother was standing at the window, peering out into the darkness, and her two sisters were huddled in the bed the three of them shared, wrapped in a blanket.

"Tis' nay good, oh, where is he?" her mother exclaimed, wringing her hands.

"He'll be back soon, Mother. Perhaps he's called at Uncle Brendan's croft. Tis' on the way back across the moorland," Hannah replied.

She was seven years old, the oldest of three sisters, and lived with her mother and father in a croft, high on the moorlands above the Balmoral estate. It was a hard life, and food was often scarce. Their father worked hard to provide for them but would often slip out at night to poach from the estate–fish from the river, or game from the forest.

"He said he'd come straight back. Look at the rain, tis' drivin' against the windows. Oh, John, where are ye?" Hannah's mother, Mary, exclaimed, turning to Hannah with tears in her eyes.

Hannah knew her mother hated her father going out poaching. She often warned him against doing so, but his response was always the same.

"We must eat, Mary, and these aristocrats have more than enough on their estates. A salmon to them is just another catch, but to us... it's life or death," he would say as he left the croft on another evening expedition.

It had been the same that night, and after a meagre supper shared with the family, he had wrapped himself in his cloak and gone out into the night.

Hannah's mother had lit candles around the croft – she could never settle whilst her husband was out poaching–and she, Hannah, and the two younger sisters had waited for his return. That had been four hours ago, and still he had not returned.

"It'll be all right, Mother. He always comes home," Hannah said, going to join her mother at the window. And just then, a light appeared in the distance, bobbing up and down across the moorland.

"Oh, thank the Lord. He's back," Hannah's mother exclaimed, but Hannah was curious–her father never took a lantern with him on his evening expeditions, and now another appeared, and another, small balls of light bobbing through the darkness.

"Tis' a party comin' towards the croft, Mother," Hannah said, and her mother hurried to the door.

"John, is that ye?" she called out into the darkness, as the rain came driving in from outside, and the wind howled so that the candles guttered and the fire in the hearth spluttered.

"Mary, tis' Brendan," the voice of Hannah's uncle called back, and Hannah went to join her mother at the door, peering out into the darkness.

The lanterns were coming closer now, and Hannah could make out the shape of several men through the darkness. They were carrying something between them, and she strained her eyes to make it out.

"Brendan? What's happened? Is it… oh, nay, it cannae be," Hannah's mother cried out in anguish, and Hannah clutched at her, as now the figures came into sight.

Hannah's uncle was leading them, and behind him came four other men–crofters from nearby dwellings. They were carrying a body wrapped in a blanket, each holding a corner, the face now visible as the head lolled over the side.

It was Hannah's father, dead and lifeless. Her mother screamed and rushed forward, throwing herself onto the muddy ground outside the croft, as the four men set down the body. Hannah stared at in disbelief, and behind her now appeared her two sisters–Maeve and Caitlin.

"What's happened?" Maeve, the eldest of the two, asked.

"Go back inside," their uncle said, as their mother clutched at the lifeless body of their father, but Hannah was rooted to the spot.

She could not move, but only stare at her father's pale, lifeless face, illuminated in the lantern light, whilst the rain fell heavily around them. She could not understand what had happened, and why he was dead. He had left the croft in high spirits, telling them he would return with a magnificent salmon for the meal the following day.

"It'll be the largest I've ever caught," he had said–he always promised that.

"Why, Brendan? What happened? Oh, dear John, my dear John," Hannah's mother exclaimed, clutching at the body, shaking it as though willing him to wake.

"He was chased, Mary–the gamekeepers on the estate caught him poachin' in the river. The rain swelled the waters. He lost his footin' and fell. They saw him go under and he was washed up half a mile downstream. They knew he was my brother and came runnin' for me. I'm so sorry, Mary," Hannah's uncle said, kneeling in the mud next to her and putting his arm around her.

"All for a salmon. They chased him for a salmon. Oh, cruel, wicked men," Hannah's mother exclaimed, sobbing uncontrollably as Hannah and her two sisters looked on.

"Let's get ye inside, Mary. Come on, lads, lift again," Hannah's uncle said, nodding to the other men, who had remained silent.

The blanket was lifted, and the body taken into the croft and laid on the bed. Hannah stood watching as her mother kneeled at the bedside, clutching at her husband's hand.

"Oh, John, what will we dae without ye? All for a salmon," she kept repeating.

"We'll be goin' now, Brendan," one of the men said, and Hannah's uncle looked up and nodded.

"Aye, thank ye, lads. Ye've done us a service this night and make nay mistake," he replied.

The men filed out, offering their condolences to Hannah's mother, and shaking their heads. The rain was still driving against the windows, and Hannah went to stand next to her mother, placing her hand gently on her shoulder.

"Mother?" she said, and her mother turned and put her arm around her.

"Oh, Hannah, oh, what are we goin' to dae? Yer poor father… I cannae…" she began, and she burst into fresh sobs, clutching at Hannah, who had tears rolling down her cheeks.

Maeve and Caitlin were standing watching, and it seemed they did not understand fully what had happened. Did they think their father would wake up? Hannah glanced at him, lying motionless on the bed.

She had seen a dead body before–that of her grandfather, who had died when Hannah was very young. But his death had been from old age, and he had been laid out in an open coffin for the crofters to pay their respects before his funeral.

This was different–her father's face was pale, his lips blue, his eyes closed, a bruise had formed on his cheek. Hannah could hardly bear to look at him–this was not her father, with his kindly smile and bright eyes, who had always told her how much he loved her and her sisters before leaving each day to follow his sheep across the moorland.

"Tis' those gamekeepers and their masters who're responsible for this," Hannah's uncle said, shaking his head.

"All for a salmon," Hannah's mother replied, as fresh tears rolled down her cheeks.

"What happens now, Mother?" Hannah asked, still clinging to her mother, who kissed her on the forehead and tightened her embrace around her.

"We carry on, Hannah. We dae what yer father would've wanted us to dae. We try to be brave, even though we'll miss him every day. Yer father was the best of men, Hannah, and he dinnae deserve this. But… oh, we'll never forget him, I promise," she said, and any further words were lost in her sobs.

At length, Hannah's uncle made her, and her three sisters go to bed, but none of them could sleep, and they watched as he and their mother kept vigil at the bedside.

"Is Father goin' to wake up?" Caitlin, who was only three years old, asked.

"Nay, Caitlin, he will nae. He's in heaven now, and we must be thankful for that," Hannah replied, remembering something the minister had said at her grandfather's funeral.

But try as she might, Hannah could not be comforted by that knowledge. Her father was gone, and she knew life would never be the same for any of them again. It was a most terrible tragedy, and she could only share her mother's bitterness at the thought of how needlessly her father had died. It had all been for a salmon–a meal for his family–and their greed and arrogance had snatched the very life from them all.

"I'll never forget ye, Father," she vowed as she closed her eyes and tried to go to sleep, her mother's sobs continuing as that dreadful night drew on, and the hope of a happy dawn was lost.

CRATHIE KIRK

Rain soon turned to snow on the moorlands above Balmoral, and the day of Hannah's father's funeral brought with it bleak, unforgiving weather, as the family huddled inside the croft, waiting for the procession to the church.

Hannah's father's coffin stood on biers in the centre of the room, and her uncle, aunt, and cousin had joined Hannah, her mother, and her two sisters as they waited for the pallbearers. It would be a simple funeral, presided over by the minster, Reverend Macreedy, and many of the crofters from the surrounding moorland would be there.

"I still cannae believe he's gone," Hannah's Aunt Rose said.

She was a dour-faced woman, and was dressed in black, with a shawl wrapped around her shoulders. She stood next to Hannah's uncle, a fine figure of a man–the very image of his brother, Hannah's father, with red hair and green eyes. He was dressed in tweed, with black breeches, and next to him stood Hannah's cousin, Connor, a youth of sixteen who also resembled Hannah's father and uncle.

"All for a salmon," Hannah's mother said, shaking her head.

She put her hand on the coffin. There were tears in her eyes, and Hannah slipped her hand into her mother's and squeezed it.

"It's all right, Mother," she said, but her mother shook her head.

"Nay, Hannah, it's nae all right. Yer father should be here with us–nae in a wooden box waitin' to be carried to the church. Tis' those wicked beasts in that castle," she said, glancing over her shoulder in the direction of Balmoral.

There had been much excitement in the surrounding district at the news: the small hunting lodge–known grandly as Balmoral Castle–had been leased by none other than the Queen and Prince Albert. Prince Albert had been seen in the vicinity, and the Queen herself was currently visiting the castle.

There were plans for acquisition, and a new, far grander residence was thought to be intended. But all of this had come at a cost, and Hannah's father had paid the price of new rules about poaching on the estate.

In the past, the landowner, Lord Farquharson, had turned a blind eye to a salmon or a brace of game birds, but the gamekeepers now–the ghillies–had been instructed to put a stop to it.

"Now, Mary, daenae upset yerself," Hannah's uncle said.

A knock now came at the door, and Hannah's aunt opened it to reveal the pallbearers waiting outside. Snow was falling, and the moorland stretched out in a fast swathe across the hillside, running down to woods and the river below.

Balmoral itself was just visible through the trees, a mile or so to the east, and as the coffin began its procession, Hannah, too, felt that same sense of bitterness at her father's loss.

"I am the resurrection, and the life; he that believeth in me, though he were dead, yet shall he live; And whosoever liveth and believeth in me shall never die," one of the men said, reading from scripture as the sad procession made its way along the moorland track from the croft.

Hannah walked with her mother, holding her hand, with

Maeve and Caitlin at her side. They were followed by Hannah's uncle, aunt, and cousin, and several of their neighbours who had come to join the procession.

It was still snowing, and the cortege wound its way down the hillside and through woodland, where the trees stood stark and bare, approaching the church, whose squat spire could be seen rising in the distance.

"Yer father loved to see the moorland covered in snow," Hannah's mother said.

"I miss him, Mother," Hannah whispered, and her mother squeezed her hand.

"Be strong, Hannah. That's what he'd want of us," she said, as the procession now came to the open gates of the church.

The minister was waiting on the steps to receive them, dressed in his simple gown and preaching bands. He took up the words from the scriptures as they approached.

"I know that my Redeemer liveth, and that he shall stand at the latter day upon the earth. And though after my skin worms destroy this body, yet in my flesh shall I see God; whom I shall see for myself, and mine eyes shall behold, and nae another," he said, as the procession came to a halt.

The minister came to greet Hannah's mother with a few words of comfort, and then the procession took up once again, making its way into the simple interior of the church, which had been the setting for so many joys and sorrows in that remote community over the years.

Hannah had been baptised there, her parents had been married there, and now her father would be buried there in the churchyard. The grave had been dug, and when the simple service was concluded, the coffin was lowered into the ground.

Hannah watched, clinging to her mother's hand, as tears rolled down her cheeks.

"I want Father," Caitlin whispered, and Hannah put her arm around her.

"It's all right, Caitlin. He's watching down on us," she said, as the minster concluded the words of burial and others stepped forward to pay their last respects.

A cold wind was blowing, and Hannah shivered, huddling close to her mother, who was weeping uncontrollably.

"Come now, Mary. Ye'll catch yer death of cold. We should be goin' home now," Hannah's aunt said, putting her arm around Hannah's mother and trying to lead her away.

"I daenae want to leave him here. All alone in the cold ground," Hannah's mother sobbed.

"He's with the good Lord now. Tis' a comfort to know that," Hannah's aunt replied.

Eventually, Hannah, her mother, and sisters were led away. It was hard for Hannah to leave her father. There was so much she wanted to say to him. She wanted to tell him she loved him, just as he had so often told her the same.

"But nay comfort for us left here. I daenae know what we'll dae? How can we live without him?" Hannah's mother exclaimed.

Her aunt had no reply for this, but she led Hannah's mother away, and Hannah and her two sisters followed. They walked out of the church gates and down the steps to the track leading back up onto the moorlands.

The river was visible through the trees. It was in flood and raging in a torrent. It made Hannah shudder to think of her father caught in its current, and she turned away, hardly able to look at it as tears welled up in her eyes.

As they began to climb up through the trees, the sound of horses on the road below caused Hannah to look up. She could see a carriage, driven by liveried footmen, and decorated in red and gold.

"Who rides in a carriage like that?" Caitlin asked, and Hannah shook her head and clenched her fists.

"Tis' the royal carriage–the Queen or one of the princesses, perhaps," she said, in a bitter tone.

She could not help but blame the occupants of the carriage – whoever they were – for her father's death. Further details had emerged in the days following the accident. Her father had slipped on a rock and fallen into the torrent after one of the gamekeepers – the ghillies – had shot at him, causing him to startle.

"Are they comin' to see us?" Caitlin asked, and Hannah shook her head.

"Nay, Caitlin. The likes of them daenae come to see the likes of us. We're poor, they're rich. And the rich always take from the poor," Hannah replied.

They walked in silence up the path through the woods. The other mourners had gone their own way, and only Hannah, her mother, her two sisters, her aunt, uncle, and cousin walked together.

"Tis' a sad day," Hannah's uncle kept repeating, and he shook his head and sighed as they emerged from the treeline onto the moor.

The wind was driving the snow into drifts, and they had to walk bent almost double against the ferocity of the storm, which now whipped itself up into a frenzy.

"Hurry now, we must get inside," Hannah's aunt called out, and the party hurried towards the croft.

They arrived, breathless, and covered in snow, and Hannah's mother ushered them inside, where all of them huddled around a hastily lit fire. It was freezing cold, and there was little to eat save a side of bacon boiled into a simple soup with vegetables and bread, which Hannah's aunt now set in a pan over the fire to warm.

"There now, tis' over–the worst is over," she said, glancing around at them and trying to put on a brave face.

But in Hannah's mind, the worst was yet to come. It had been her father who had provided for them. Her mother had taken care of Hannah and her two sisters, whilst her father had farmed the sheep and sold their wool and meat at the market in nearby Ballater. It had been a simple existence, but one they had been happy in – until now.

"But I daenae know what we'll dae now. I'll have to take in mendin' or sew garments for sale. But I daenae know…" Hannah's mother said, glancing at Hannah and shaking her head.

"Daenae think about all that today, Mary. Yer grievin' John's loss," Hannah's uncle said as he put a piece of wood on the fire and held out his hands to warm them.

"But how can we put food on the table? How can I feed the children?" she said, glancing at Hannah and her sisters.

"We'll find a way, I promise ye," Hannah's uncle replied.

The soup was bubbling in the pan, and Hannah's aunt began to serve it. But as she handed Hannah a bowl, the sound of horse's hooves outside caused them all to look up.

It was growing dark now, and the path across the moorland would be treacherous in the snow. Hannah glanced at her mother, and her uncle went to the door, taking up a lantern and opening it cautiously.

"Who goes there?" he called out into the night.

"An equerry of Her Majesty," came the response, and all of them looked at one another in surprise.

"And what would Her Majesty want with us? Hasn't she already done enough damage?" Hannah's mother said, as she went to join her brother-in-law at the door.

Hannah and her sisters peered out of the window. The moon had appeared from behind the clouds, and it had stopped snowing, so that a silvery light was cast over the moorland.

Hannah could see the horse and rider, and now the man dismounted and came to greet her mother and uncle at the door. He was dressed in livery and wrapped in a cloak. His accent was that of the British establishment–clipped and formal. He nodded to Hannah's mother and uncle before addressing them.

"I bring Her Majesty's condolences on the death of your

husband. Her Majesty witnessed the sad sight of the burial from her carriage this afternoon and asked to know the details of your husband's death. On learning of what happened, she wishes to extend you her heartfelt condolences, and offers this token in reparation," the man said.

He turned back to the horse, which was saddled with two large saddlebags, and from these he produced several items which he presented to Hannah's mother, who stared at them in astonishment.

"But… what are these?" she asked, and the equerry looked at her in surprise.

"Goods, madam–a caddy of tea, a side of bacon, a cheese, bread, preserves, and other items which Her Majesty hopes will go some way to alleviating your current troubles," the man replied.

"Is that so? Well, ye can thank Her Majesty kindly, and tell her a side of bacon will nae help bring back my husband," Hannah's mother exclaimed, and she turned and marched back into the croft, leaving the equerry standing at the door.

"Mary…" Hannah's uncle said, but Hannah's mother had sunk into a chair by the hearth and was sobbing.

"Her Majesty also asks me to inform you of the planned building works at Balmoral. She understands John had a nephew, and a brother, whom I presume is yourself, and I am to tell you that work will soon be available for those in need of a job," the equerry replied continued.

"That's very kind of ye. Aye, my son, Connor, and I… we shall all of us need work in the comin' months," Hannah's uncle replied.

"Then I suggest you make yourselves known at the estate office in due course," the equerry replied, and bidding them goodnight, he climbed into the saddle and rode off across the moor.

Hannah's uncle closed the door and turned to Hannah's mother, shaking his head.

"Ye should've shown him some respect, Mary. Tis' the Queen herself who sends these gifts," he said, glancing at the table, where Hannah's aunt had laid out the food sent from Balmoral.

Hannah's mother looked up at him angrily.

"A side of bacon? A caddy of tea? A loaf of bread? What's that to her? She will nae miss it. My husband–yer brother–died because of her and her gamekeepers. Does she think a few raised pies and a side of cheese can make up for that?" she replied, shaking her head.

"And she offers Connor and I a job. She cares, Mary," Hannah's uncle replied, but Hannah's mother was having none of it.

"Give me back my husband. That's all I want. Nothin' more than that," she said, wiping her eyes with a handkerchief.

Hannah went over to her and put her arms around her. She shared her mother's anger against the estate and all it stood for.

Her father would still be alive if it were not for the cruel way in which the gamekeepers had behaved. Her mother was right–a caddy of tea and a side of bacon would not make up for their loss, and neither would the prospect of a job for Connor or her uncle.

"Ye must try to eat somethin' though, Mother. Ye'll be nay good to anyone if ye daenae," Hannah whispered, still with her arms around her mother's neck.

Her mother nodded and gave a weak smile.

"Ye've always been such a good lass, Hannah. I know ye'll take good care of yer mother and yer sisters, will ye nae?" she said, as Hannah's aunt sliced a piece of bread from the loaf and spread it with butter.

"I will, Mother. I promise," Hannah replied.

"We'll get through this–if Connor and I take jobs on the estate, we'll…" Hannah's uncle began, but her mother interrupted.

"And betray yer brother's memory?" she demanded, but Hannah's uncle now became angry.

"What choice dae we have?" he demanded, and he banged his fist down on the table.

Hannah began to cry. Tears rolled down her cheeks, and she turned away from her mother and ran to the bed, throwing herself beneath the blankets and sobbing.

"There, now, Brendan. Look what ye've done. Ye've upset the children," Hannah's mother exclaimed, as now Maeve and Caitlin began to cry.

"I'm only tryin' to help, Mary. If my brother hadn't been such a…" Hannah's uncle began, but her mother interrupted him.

"A fool? That's what ye were goin' to say, Brendan. Aye, a fool–a fool for tryin' to take care of his family, fool for poachin' on the estate, a fool for lovin' us," she cried.

"Please stop, please," Hannah cried out, turning to them with an imploring look on her face.

She desperately wanted her father. She missed him more than words could say. But he was gone, and he was not coming back. She had tried to explain it to her sisters, but neither of them had fully understood.

She looked at the empty chair by the hearth and imagined what her father would say if he could hear them arguing as they were.

"Aye, Brendan–stop this. Let's all have somethin' to eat and then go to bed," Hannah's aunt said.

Her uncle nodded and made no further comment. They ate their soup in silence, and Hannah's aunt handed around pieces of cake which the Queen had sent them. It tasted delicious–a rich fruit cake with marzipan–but Hannah hardly noticed.

She could think only of her father, and the sad tragedy of his loss. Life would never be the same for any of them again–not now that an empty chair stood in the corner. Her father's hat hung on the hook by the door. He had not taken it with him on the night he died–a strange omission, for he always had his hat on his head when out of doors.

"Try to sleep, my precious children," Hannah's mother said, as she bid Hannah and her sisters goodnight.

Hannah's aunt was already asleep in the chair by the fire, and her uncle and cousin had taken the bed belonging to Hannah's mother and father.

"Will ye lie with us tonight, Mother?" Hannah whispered as her mother pulled the blankets and climbed in next to her.

"Aye, Hannah, I will, and we'll say our prayers together as we always dae," her mother replied.

They always said their prayers last thing at night, but Hannah did not know what to ask for or what to be thankful for that day. The hope she longed for–that her father would return–was a prayer she knew would not be answered, and she could find nothing to thank God for on that dark night when the wind howled around the croft, and all seemed hopeless.

"I daenae know what to pray for, Mother," Hannah whispered, closing her eyes, and putting her hands together.

"Then pray for me, Hannah, that I can take care of ye, and yer sisters," her mother replied, and that was just what Hannah did, before falling into a broken sleep, as she longed for her father's return.

BALMORAL CASTLE

Spring came late to the moorlands, and the thaw was slow to set in. It had been a hard winter, and the family had eked out an existence amidst the harsh and unforgiving landscape.

Hannah's aunt, uncle, and cousin had moved into the croft, and together the family had supported one another, the women taking in mending, whilst Brendan and Connor had tended the sheep and sought work on the nearby farms. But times were hard, and the crofter's way of life was changing with the arrival of the royal household at Balmoral.

Christmas had been a miserable affair with little joy or celebration, and there had been no cheer in the meagre meal they had shared to celebrate the feast.

"I'll be glad when the spring comes," Hannah's mother had said.

But the arrival of spring had brought with it little hope of respite. Times were still hard, and reluctantly, Hannah's uncle and cousin were forced to take up the offer of labouring on the new construction of Balmoral Castle.

"Why dae they need to make the house bigger? Is it nae big

enough already? Balmoral was a fine house in days gone by," Hannah's mother said, shaking her head, as Hannah's uncle and cousin prepared to make the walk to the estate office on the first day of their work for the royal household.

"Prince Albert wants a castle fit for his Queen. The design includes a tower, and new stables. It'll be quite magnificent when it's finished," Hannah's uncle replied.

Her mother tutted and shook her head. Hannah was helping her aunt with her weaving, and she looked up at her cousin, who was pulling on his boots.

"Dae ye want to work there, Connor?" she asked, for Hannah shared her mother's disapproval of the estate.

It had been a source of argument in the family ever since the day of her father's death – Hannah and her mother blamed the estate for the events leading to his death, whilst her uncle was willing to put the matter behind them. It was a stalemate, and now her cousin looked up and sighed.

"What would ye have me dae, Hannah? I cannae sit idly here and have nay work, can I?" he replied.

Hannah liked her cousin. He was hardworking and was always trying to better himself. He had taught himself to read from the Bible and had ambitions to be an engineer in the tradition of Isambard Kingdom Brunel.

"We've got to dae somethin'–we've nay money comin' in," Hannah's uncle replied, and he beckoned to Connor to follow him.

Hannah watched them leave, glancing at her mother, who shook her head.

"Betrayin' his memory, that's what they're doin'–it'll come to a sorry end," she said, returning to her mending.

Hannah's aunt remained resolutely quiet, and Hannah knew better than to say anything. It had not been easy for the family to come together under one roof, but Hannah knew her aunt and uncle were struggling–just as she and her mother and sisters were, too. It made sense for them to live together in the larger of the two crofts, but familial bonds did not make for harmonious living, and there had been many arguments and fallings out in the weeks and months since they had come to live together.

"Dae Uncle Brendan and Connor work for the Queen?" Maeve asked.

"Aye, Maeve, they dae. But be quiet for now," Hannah whispered, watching, as her mother concentrated hard on her mending, and knowing such talk would only lead to further upset.

PRINCE ALBERT HAD plans for a magnificent new castle at Balmoral. It would take several years to complete and required dozens of hands to labour at the work. Hannah's uncle and cousin were amongst them, and as spring gave way to summer, and the heathers turned the moorland deep shades of purple and gold, work on the castle continued.

Hannah did what she could to help her mother and aunt, taking care of her sisters, and running errands as was necessary.

"Oh, yer uncle's forgotten the food I prepared for him, and Connor, too," Hannah's aunt exclaimed one morning.

She had wrapped bread and cheese for each of them in muslin, along with a bag of apples from the store at the side of the croft.

"I can take it for them. I know the way to the castle like the back of my hand," Hannah said.

She had spent her life roaming the moors, following her father and the sheep. She knew every path, every crag, every stream crossing, and could find her way as much in the light as in the dark. Her aunt looked over at Hannah's mother, who nodded.

"Aye, let her go. She can call on Professor Lochray on the way back with his mendin'–I have it here ready," Hannah's mother said, and she beckoned Hannah over and handed her a pair of folded breeches, the hems of which had been neatly stitched.

"I will nae be long, Mother," Hannah said, and her mother smiled.

"Take yer time, lass. Tis' good to run across the moorland and feel the fresh summer breeze in yer hair, and the scent of the heathers in yer nostrils. Off ye go," she said, and Hannah took the food and the breeches and hurried out of the croft.

It was a beautiful day, the wide, blue sky opening a vista across the moorland. Hannah could see for many miles in every direction, and she took a path leading across the heathers and down into the glen, through the trees.

She liked to be alone with her thoughts, and she walked quietly and purposefully, pausing on a rocky outcrop to gaze down at a gushing waterfall below. There, standing proudly by the water's edge, was a stag – a magnificent monarch of the glen. Hannah smiled and crouched down amongst the ferns to watch it.

She had always delighted in seeing the animals who roamed the woods and moorlands. Her father had taught her to track them, showing her the signs and pointing out the trails of the animals – like the stag – who could be followed for miles if only one knew how.

"You're magnificent," she said to herself as the stag lowered its head to drink.

But at that moment, a shot rang out, and the stag looked up in alarm. In a moment, it was gone, retreating into the trees, as another shot rang out.

"Did you see it, Johnson? Marvellous creature. Imagine its head on the wall of the club," a voice called out, and Hannah watched as two men, clad in tweeds and carrying rifles, emerged from the trees.

Hannah was well hidden above amongst the ferns, and she watched sadly as the two men ran off in the direction the stag had taken. She knew what would happen–they would follow that magnificent creature for miles across the moorland, waiting for the perfect moment to strike. The stag would die–not for its meat, or to feed a hungry family, but for sport. Her father had abhorred such practices.

"Take only what ye need from nature," he had often said, and whilst he would poach game birds and fish to feed the family, he would never have countenanced shooting for sport.

Hannah shook her head and sighed, rising from amidst the ferns and carrying on along the path in the direction of the castle.

The new house was rising from a position close to the river, where new trees had been planted and a garden was being laid out. It was being built of granite, the grey stones hued from quarries nearby, and pulled to the site by horses. A baronial looking tower was almost finished, and a new wing was being built to one side, so that the house would be a magnificent dwelling once it was finished.

Hannah could hear the shouts of men as she approached, and she watched with interest as a large piece of stone was hauled into place, ready to be winched up onto scaffolding above.

"Easy there, McGinn, watch yerself," a man called out as another steadied the winch.

Hannah looked around for her uncle or cousin. She could see Connor on the scaffolding above, and now she spotted her uncle, talking with one of the foremen, the two of them examining a large plan which the other was holding unfurled.

"Hannah? What are ye doin' here?" her uncle asked as Hannah approached.

"Ye forget yer midday meal, Uncle," Hannah replied, holding up the wrapped bread and cheese.

Her uncle smiled.

"And they sent ye down to bring it, did they? Well, ye are a good lass and make nay mistake," her uncle said, smiling at Hannah as he took the bread and cheese from her.

Connor had spotted her, and he climbed down from the scaffolding and came over to greet her.

"I knew I'd forgotten somethin'–my stomach was just startin' to rumble, too," he said, grinning at Hannah, who smiled.

Her cousin had always been kind to her, and he was more a brother than a cousin, even as she found being there at the castle difficult. The men in the forest, the extravagance of wealth all around her – it was all a reminder of why her father had died. He had only wanted to feed his family, but even the loss of a single salmon was too much for the royal household to accept.

"Mother sent me out – I'm to deliver some mendin' to Professor Lochray on the way back," Hannah said.

Her cousin was about to reply when the sounds of a carriage caused them all to look up. The driveway from the castle led down to a bridge over the river, and through the trees an ornate carriage appeared, emblazoned with the crest of the Duke of Braemar, appeared.

The Duke of Braemear was a local nobleman, whose estate bordered that of Balmoral. He was a wealthy man, but it was well known he preferred his wealth to be spent on horses and gambling than on good works towards those who lived on his estate.

"The duke's been placed in charge of the buildin' work. He's come to review our progress," Hannah's uncle said as the workers lined up to greet the duke, who came in the name of the Queen and Prince Albert.

The carriage pulled up outside the half-finished house and a footman climbed down to open the compartment door. Hannah watched with interest. She had never seen the Duke of Braemar before, though she had heard her mother talk of him in much the same manner she spoke of the Royal Family.

"Good day, yer grace. Tis' an honour to welcome ye," the foreman said, hurrying forward to greet the duke, who nodded and waved his hand.

He was a stout man with a portly face who wore half-moon spectacles and a knee-length frock coat, stiff collar, shirt, and breeches. He looked around him approvingly and nodded.

"I wanted to see your progress. It all looks to be going well," he said, clambering down from the carriage.

Behind him, Hannah was surprised to catch a glimpse of a boy–no older than herself, who gazed up at the tower above and then at the workers still lined up quietly in front. He had fair hair and soft cheeks and was dressed in much the same way as the duke.

"We're making excellent headway, yer grace. We'll have the buildin' finished in nay time. Tis' an honour to serve their majesties," the foreman said.

"I've brought my nephew with me. I want him to see hard work in progress," the duke said, as the foreman now led him on an inspection.

Hannah watched the duke's nephew with interest. He had an arrogant look about him and looked around him with something resembling disdain. His eyes fell on Hannah for a moment, and whilst she forced herself to smile, he viewed her with only passing interest.

"I'm sure ye'll agree, yer grace–tis' a house fit for their majesties," the foreman said, as the duke looked around him and nodded.

"It certainly will be. A highland retreat, away from the hustle and bustle of London. I'm sure their majesties will be quite happy here," he said, and the foreman nodded.

"Aye, yer grace, I'm sure they will," he said.

The duke made further inspections, commenting on the layout of the gardens, and giving some instructions as to how long he expected the work to take. It seemed the Queen and Prince Albert were keen to take possession of their new home as soon as possible, and more workers were to be employed from the surrounding area to ensure the house was finished on time.

"Why did they choose to come here?" Hannah asked, for she found it remarkable to think of the Queen and Prince Albert choosing such a remote corner of the highlands, when they had all that London surely had to offer, and any number of other palaces and dwellings to choose from.

"They like our way of life, they like the highlands," her uncle replied, as the duke and his nephew climbed into the waiting carriage.

Hannah thought this to be a very odd thing to say, for it was not *their* way of life the Queen and her husband would experience, but their own vision of it–shooting stags and travelling around by carriage, ghillies balls and picnics on the moorlands.

That was no highland life–not as Hannah and her family knew it, at least.

"I'm sure they'll be very happy here," Hannah replied, even as she dreaded the day the royal party would return.

She knew how much it upset her mother to think of what had happened because of the ghillies and the royal estate. She would never forgive them for the tragedy, and Hannah felt certain she, too, would always hold an animosity towards the Queen, who, despite having offered her condolences, had done little more to alleviate the family's troubles.

"A strange child – the duke's nephew. I cannae see the likes of him ever wantin' to dae a day's work, can ye?" Hannah's cousin said, shaking his head as he unwrapped his bread and cheese.

"These aristocrats are all the same — good at inspectin' what others dae and passin' their comments on it. Well, Hannah, ye should get goin'–thank yer aunt for the food, and we'll see ye later," Hannah's uncle said, and Hannah bid them goodbye and set off back through the forest and onto the moorland.

Professor Lochray's croft lay half a mile to the west of the castle, off the path, a climb up onto the crag. He was a kindly man, very bookish, who had come from Edinburgh to study butterflies on the heathers.

Hannah had met him one afternoon in early spring, sitting with a large net by a large gorse bush. He had told her about a particular butterfly he was hunting, and that if he found it, he would become famous amongst his colleagues at the university and beyond.

She found him sitting in a chair outside the croft, drawing a picture of his latest find, and he looked up at her and smiled.

"Ah, good day to ye, Hannah, my dear. Have ye brought my breeches? Yer mother's done a fine job, I'm sure. I've another pair for her, if ye'll take them. I was leapin' across one of the streams yesterday, tryin' to catch a particularly beautiful Marsh Fritillary and the seam tore clean in two," he said, laughing, as he closed his sketchbook.

Hannah smiled. Professor Lochray always had a tale to tell. He intended to spend the summer in the highlands before returning to Edinburgh to write up his findings into a paper he hoped to publish, a paper he had told Hannah would make him famous.

"I can take it for ye now, professor. I'm sure my mother can repair it," Hannah replied.

"I'm sure she can–but can she repair my embarrassment?" he asked, laughing at his own joke.

"But did ye catch it?" Hannah asked, and the professor nodded.

"Oh, aye, and a fine specimen tis' - would ye like to see?" he asked, and he beckoned Hannah into the croft, which was filled with all manner of displays of the butterfly collector's art.

The Marsh Fritillary was in a jar, flapping around, and the professor held the jar up to the light for Hannah to see.

"Tis' beautiful," Hannah said, and the professor nodded.

"The natural world is–I've never understood man's propensity for destroyin' so much of it. I heard them shootin' again today. Tis' nay wonder the butterflies all fly away," the professor said, shaking his head.

"I saw them shootin'—there was a stag. I hope they did nae get it," Hannah said, and the professor nodded.

"Aye, alas, they always dae in the end. But thank yer mother for her kindness. Here's the payment, and a little extra, too. Will ye stay and have tea with me? I've had some supplies sent up from Ballater. There's a fruit cake, and a raised pie," he said, and Hannah nodded.

She knew her mother would scold her for being late home, but to spend an hour with the professor and forget her troubles as he talked of his adventures was worth the telling off. She sat down at the table, watching the butterfly in its jar, and imagining herself flying away across the heathers.

"I'd like to be a butterfly," she said, and the professor laughed.

"A butterfly has to endure somethin' ugly before it becomes somethin' beautiful," he said, smiling at her as he placed a large piece of cake in front of her.

A TERRIBLE DAY

"And daenae forget yer bread and cheese," Hanna's aunt called out, as her uncle and cousin got ready for work that morning.

It was late spring, and work on the new house was progressing rapidly. It would not be long before some of the quarters were habitable, and there was talk of Prince Albert himself coming to inspect the progress made.

Hannah was helping her mother with her weaving, and she looked up and smiled at her cousin, who was trying not to laugh.

"We will nae forget, Mother," he said, as she handed him a piece of muslin wrapped around his food.

"The sooner the place is finished, the better," Hannah's mother muttered.

She had grudgingly come to accept the necessity of her brother-in-law and nephew working on the construction of the castle, even as she continued to blame the Royal Family for Hannah's father's death. Hannah, too, sided with her mother in the matter, and whilst they could not do without the money, she would be only too glad when the building work was finished.

"And what are we goin' to dae when tis' finished? Will ye find work for us here and pay us a fair wage?" Hannah's uncle replied.

Her mother waved her hand dismissively–it was an old argument, and one which had long ago reached a stalemate.

"Ye'll find somethin'–and it'll be better than workin' for them," she said.

"I've been told I could be a groom in the stables if I work hard, or one of the ghillies, even," Connor said.

Hannah glanced up at him even as he realised he had said the wrong thing. Hannah's mother stared at him angrily.

"A ghillie? Yer ambition is to be a ghillie? And will ye be shootin' poachers, too, Connor?" she demanded.

"Let's go, now," Hannah's uncle said, and he ushered Connor out of the croft.

Hannah's mother tutted and shook her head. There were tears in her eyes, and Hannah knew how hurt she would be if Connor took up such an offer, even as it was a remarkable opportunity.

The morning passed in awkward silence. Hannah's two sisters were being taught to help with the mending, though at three years old, Caitlin could do little more than sort the piles of clothes into different types, whilst Maeve was continually pricking her finger with the needles as she attempted to follow their mother's lead in stitching.

"Ye cannae dae it like that, Maeve," Hannah said, threading her sister's needle for the tenth time that morning.

Her aunt, who had remained quiet throughout, now looked up and shook her head.

"Let them go out to play. They're a hindrance, nae a help," she said, and Hannah's mother nodded.

"Aye, they can go out–but nay further than the east cairn," she said.

The east cairn was a pile of stones which lay around half a mile from the croft. It marked the furthest extremity of the

Balmoral estate, and beyond it lay open moorland stretching for miles towards the high mountains in the west.

"Did ye hear that?" Hannah said, and her two sisters nodded.

They put on their shawls and went out to play, leaving Hannah, her mother, and aunt in the croft. It was quiet, save for the clacking on the spinning wheel, and the gentle buzz of a bee who had entered through the open window.

"We used to sing to pass the time. Dae ye remember, Mary?" Hannah's aunt asked, and Hannah's mother looked up and nodded.

"Aye, I remember. But tis' hard to sing when ye've nay song in yer heart," she replied.

Hannah remembered those days fondly. Her mother had a beautiful voice, and she would sing songs of bygone days, of men and women falling in love, and of romance amongst the heathers.

But since the death of Hannah's father, her mother's song had fallen silent, and it was as though the soul of the house itself was gone.

"One day, perhaps," Hannah's aunt replied, and they returned to their weaving.

The morning passed as it did every day. Hannah helped her mother with the mending. She had become adept with needle and thread and could stitch and repair with the skill of one twice her age.

She was glad to be helping her mother and doing her bit to make ends meet. Life had never been so hard for any of them, but together, they were doing all they could to support one another.

"I'll make the walk to Ballater tomorrow–there's things we need," Hannah's aunt said, sitting back from the spinning wheel and rising to her feet.

"We'll all go. Tis' a pleasant time of year to walk across the moorland," Hannah's mother said, but as she spoke, the door flew open, and Maeve and Caitlin appeared, with tears in their eyes.

"Whatever's the matter? What's happened to ye?" Hannah's mother exclaimed.

"Oh, Mother, come quickly. Tis' Uncle Brendan. There's been an accident. Connor sent us to bring ye," Maeve cried out.

Hannah's aunt screamed, and she rushed out of the croft as Hannah and her mother followed.

"What happened? What accident?" Hannah's mother asked.

"Some stones fell from the castle. He was hit. Connor told us to run as fast as we could and bring ye," Maeve replied.

They ran along the moorland path, Hannah's aunt several paces in front. It was not long before they came in sight of the castle and Hannah could see a crowd gathered, and a carriage parked nearby. There were tears in her eyes, and already she feared the worst.

"What's happened? Where's my husband?" Hannah's aunt cried out, and she fought her way through the crowd, followed by the others.

Hannah now saw her uncle lying on the ground. Connor was at his side, and his leg was bloodied and contorted. A large piece of masonry was lying on one side, and it appeared to have fallen from a height above, crushing Hannah's uncle's leg beneath it.

He was crying out in agony, as Hannah's aunt now kneeled beside him.

"Rose, I cannae feel my leg. Tis' there, is it?" he gasped.

"Tis' there, aye, Brendan. But ye've suffered a terrible accident. Try to keep still. They'll bring the doctor. Has someone called for the doctor?" Hannah's aunt called out.

The foreman nodded and pointed to the carriage.

"The Duke of Braemar–he's sent word to Ballater. The doctor will nae be long," he said.

"And where was the Duke of Braemar when this happened? What sort of man allows an accident like this to occur?" Hannah's mother demanded.

"I assure you, madam, I've done all I can to help," a voice

behind them said, and Hannah turned to find the duke himself standing in front of them.

"And if yer kind could only live in crofts and nae these fancy houses, perhaps my brother-in-law wouldnae be lyin' with his leg crushed," Hannah's mother exclaimed, pointing her finger angrily at the duke, who seemed somewhat taken aback.

"I assure you…" he began, but Hannah's mother's anger was spilling over now, and she advanced on him, shaking her fist at him.

"Yer kind killed my husband, and now this," she exclaimed.

"Mother," Hannah whispered, catching her by the hand.

"Nay, Hannah. He needs to learn we crofters are nae just his servants to be treated with contempt," she exclaimed.

"I've sent for the doctor. I'll pay his fees, and you'll be compensated for the accident. Good day to you," the duke said, and turning on his heels, he marched back to the waiting carriage.

Hannah's mother shook her fist at him, but Hannah now pulled her back. Their attentions turned to Hannah's uncle, who was still lying in agony on the ground with her aunt trying to comfort him. At length, the doctor arrived, and the wounds were tended to. The leg was broken in several places, and a splint was fitted, and a stretcher improvised.

"I'll nae work again," Hannah's uncle kept repeating.

"Daenae worry about that. Ye heard what the duke said. We'll be compensated. Tis' all right, Brendan," Hannah's aunt said, holding her husband's hand as the stretcher was carried away from the castle.

Hannah, Maeve, Caitlin, and their mother followed, with Connor remaining behind to gather his father's things. It was another tragedy for the family—a bitter blow, just as things appeared to be settling down.

Without the income from Hannah's uncle's employment on the building work, the family would sink further into poverty. It was a terrible prospect, and one they all knew, even as only Hannah's uncle was willing to voice his fears.

"He'll dae nothin' for us–a caddy of tea and a side of bacon. That's what we got for John's death. A crushed leg is nae worth anythin' to them," he said, shaking his head as he lay back with a sigh.

The stretcher was carried by four of the workers, and they made a sorrowful procession through the woods and onto the moorland path. Hannah had hold of Maeve and Caitlin by the hands, and they followed a few paces behind their mother, who was comforting their aunt.

"Will Uncle Brendan die like Father?" Maeve asked.

Hannah scolded her.

"Daenae say such things, Maeve. Nay, Uncle Brendan will nae die. He's had a terrible accident, but he will nae die," she replied, and Maeve nodded.

"I daenae want him to die," she said, and she began to sob.

Hannah put her arm around her, and now Caitlin, too, began to cry. The two sisters, it seemed, overwhelmed by the sorrow engulfing the family. The progression along the moorland path was slow, and the stretcher bearers forced to stop several times, for the day was warm in the late spring sunshine.

Eventually, they reached the croft, and with some difficulty, Hannah's uncle was placed on the bed he shared with Hannah's aunt, behind a curtain at the back of the croft.

"I'll make some soup," Hannah's mother said, and Hannah watched as her aunt tried to make her uncle comfortable.

"How did it happen, Brendan? How did the masonry fall on ye?" she asked.

"I daenae know. It all happened so quickly. There was a shout from up above. Someone saw it dislodge. But I could nae get out of the way in time. It landed on me as I leaped to one side. It could've been worse–much worse," he replied.

Hannah shuddered to think of this, and she was thankful for

the small mercy of an accident, rather than the tragedy of a death. To lose her uncle, as well as her father, would have been unbearable. He had become a father figure to her, and she loved him dearly, just as she knew her mother and sisters did, too.

"Daenae dwell on that. Yer leg – it'll heal, and we'll manage, I'm sure," Hannah's aunt said, squeezing her husband's hand.

Hannah's mother was busying herself with the hearth, and Hannah went to help her, the two of them preparing vegetables and a piece of mutton for the soup.

"What happens now, Mother? What will we dae?" Hannah asked, but her mother shook her head.

"I daenae know, Hannah. We'll have to manage, though. It will nae be easy. We'll all of us must dae our bit–ye and yer sisters included," she said, and Hannah nodded.

"I know, Mother. I'll dae whatever I can to help," she said, and her mother gave a weak smile.

"Ye should be a child still, Hannah. But ye've been forced to grow up these months gone by. I'm proud of ye, and I know yer father would be proud of ye, too," she replied, with tears in her eyes.

Hannah nodded. She missed her father terribly. He had always had a kind word for her or a kind gesture to show her how much he loved her. Her mother was the same, but in these difficult times, it was as though she were a shadow of her former self.

Hannah missed her, too–she missed her laugh, her songs, her kind expression, all of which had been replaced by the burden of sadness.

"I miss him, Mother," she said, and her mother put her arm around her.

"And I miss him, too. But if we keep his memory alive–tis' all that matters," she replied.

* * *

In the days that followed, Hannah's uncle developed a fever. His wounds had become infected, and his temperature rose, bringing on night sweats and delusions. The family took it in turns to sit with him, trying all they could to break the fever with hot drinks and water-soaked cloths dabbed on his forehead.

"It's nay use. Nothin' works," Hannah's aunt exclaimed, shaking her head with tears in her eyes.

"It's all right, Rose. Yer doin' yer best," Hannah's mother said, but there was despair in her voice, too.

Nothing they did was working, and the fever was only getting worse. In desperation, Hannah went to visit the professor, finding him outside his croft, drawing in his sketchbook.

"Good day to ye, Hannah. I've nae seen ye these past few days. I heard about yer uncle. Is he recoverin' from his injuries?" the professor asked, closing his sketchbook as Hannah came up to him.

"Nay, professor. He's worse. A fever—we cannae dae anythin' to help him. He grows delirious. I'm afraid… oh, I daenae want him to die," she exclaimed, and promptly burst into tears.

She had tried to stay strong for her mother's sake, but now her feelings overwhelmed her. She thought of her father and imagined the pain of losing another person she loved. The professor pulled out a large red spotted handkerchief from his pocket and held it out to her.

"There, there, my dear—ye poor thing. I'm so sorry to hear about yer uncle. Sit yerself down, lass. There we are. But he's a strong man—as strong as an ox. Ye daenae have to fear for his life," the professor said, pulling a chair up next to his.

Hannah sat down and wiped her eyes.

"I'm sorry," she said, but the professor smiled.

"There's nothin' to be sorry about. Ye cry because ye care. It shows yer heart, Hannah," he said, taking her hand in his.

"But if he dies…" Hannah began, voicing the fear in her heart.

"Nay, Hannah. Ye cannae think like that. Fevers come and go.

We must let them take their course. He'll be all right, I'm sure. But he needs time to recover. It'll take a few days, weeks, perhaps. But he's got yer mother and yer aunt to take care of him. And ye, too," he replied.

Hannah nodded and looked up at him with a weak smile. She was grateful for his reassurance, even as she doubted his words.

"I... is there anythin' ye could dae for him, professor?" she asked.

The professor pondered for a moment.

"I'm nay doctor, Hannah. I study butterflies. I know nothin' of medicine, save... well, a little trainin' in my younger days at the university. I once thought about bein' a surgeon, but... well, the butterflies found me," he replied.

Hannah's face fell. The professor was the cleverest man she had ever met. The croft was filled with books, and it seemed there was no subject he was unable to converse on. He patted her hand as she looked up at with fresh tears rolling down her cheeks.

"Dae ye... can ye visit him? It might reassure him," she said, and the professor smiled.

"If it brings peace to yer heart, Hannah. Aye, I'll visit him. I've some ointment here I make from heather and honey. Tis' a balm of sorts for cuts to the hand. I'm always cuttin' myself, on thistles and gorse. Tis' a relief to bathe my hands at the end of the day. I'll take some of that–perhaps it might help," he said, and Hannah's face broke into a smile.

"Oh, thank ye, professor," she said, as the professor made his way inside the croft to fetch the ointment.

He returned with a large bottle in hand, and a box, which he told her contained a fruitcake. Together, they set off across the moors and down the hill towards Hannah's croft.

On the way, the professor pointed out all manner of plants, the names of which Hannah had never heard of before. She marvelled at the professor's knowledge, and just as they were approaching the croft, he paused and uttered a cry of exclamation.

"Oh, my, look, tis' a female hollyblue, Hannah. Look there on the heather. Is nae she beautiful?" the professor exclaimed.

He pointed towards a butterfly, and Hannah peered down at the heather, on which rested a light blue butterfly, with almost black tips at its wings.

"Will you catch her, professor?" Hannah asked, but the professor shook his head.

"I have one already in my collection. But tis' a blessin' to see one, indeed," he said, smiling at Hannah, who now watched as the butterfly fluttered off across the heathers.

Hannah now led the way to the croft, not bothering to knock at the door, and finding her mother lighting a fire in the hearth, whilst her aunt took her turn at her uncle's side. Maeve and Caitlin were sitting on the rug, and they looked up in surprise as the professor entered the croft.

Her cousin was still out at work, but Hannah's mother welcomed the professor warmly – he had been a good friend to them, despite the obvious differences which existed between them.

"Yer very kind, professor. Tis' more than ye needed to dae. I hope Hannah wasnae botherin' ye to come here today," Hannah's mother said, glancing at Hannah and raising her eyebrows.

But the professor shook his head.

"Nae, Mary. She's a delight. I enjoy her visitin' me up at my croft. I'm only too glad to be of help–if I can. The ointment will soothe yer injuries, Brendan. I know how expensive medicine can be. And I hope ye'll enjoy the cake, too," the professor replied.

Hannah's uncle and aunt thanked him profusely, and Hannah walked with him a short distance across the moorland before bidding him goodbye.

"Dae ye think the Royal Family comin' here is a good thing,

professor? It's only brought misery to my family," she said, and the professor pondered for a moment.

"Ye cannae stop them from comin' here. They've brought employment to the crofters, they've improved the roads, and nay doubt they'll dae more, too, in years to come. But I understand, Hannah – ye lost yer father because of them, and now yer uncle lies injured because of their desire for a bigger house on the estate. I daenae know the answer – only time will tell. But ye've proved yer character well enough. I'm proud to call ye my friend," he said, and smiling at her, he pulled a small tin from his pocket.

It contained toffees, and he handed it to her for her own reward. She thanked him and watched as he climbed up the towards his croft, pausing to let out a cry of delight at the sight of a butterfly he now chased.

Hannah smiled. She was grateful to him for his kindness, and she knew his words were true. The Royal Family was not entirely to blame for the sad circumstances her family now endured. Fate had played its part, too, and Hannah wondered if fate might now bring with it a happier future for them all.

SURPRISING NEWS

In the coming weeks, Hanna's uncle's condition steadily improved. The fever left him, and whilst he remained weak, the danger of death had passed.

Hannah was relieved. She had feared the worst – despite the professor's assurances – and to see her uncle regaining his strength brought her relief. She was only seven years old, but Hannah was a deep thinker, and she had seen the worried looks her mother and aunt had exchanged when her uncle had been at his worst.

But despite his recovery from the fever, his injuries from the falling masonry remained. His leg was terribly deformed. It would need an operation to set it right – one which no crofter could ever have afforded, and the expertise for which simply was not available in such a remote part of the highlands.

"Let me help ye, Father," Connor said, as Hannah's uncle tried to get up out of bed.

"Nay, lad. I need to manage myself. Let me be," Hannah's uncle said.

It was the first time he had attempted to get up out of bed, and he had pulled himself to the edge of the bed and was now trying to lift himself using a pair of crutches brought for him by the professor.

"Brendan, be careful," Hannah's aunt exclaimed, but she, too, was rebuffed, as Hannah's uncle tried to lift himself off the bed.

Hannah was helping her mother chop vegetables for a mutton stew, and now she watched as her uncle tried with all his might to lift himself. He cursed under his breath, falling back onto the bed with a sigh.

"Tis' nay use," he exclaimed, throwing the crutches to one side.

"It's yer first attempt, Father. Ye are nae strong enough yet. Let us help ye," Connor said, and Hannah's aunt nodded.

"Aye, Brendan. Let Connor help ye. A day at a time. That's what it takes. Ye cannae hope to manage it the first time. But perhaps the second or the third. Perseverance – ye'd be the first to speak of perseverance," she said.

Hannah's uncle sighed, but to everyone's relief, he allowed Connor to help him get up from the bed. With considerable effort on both their parts, Hannah's uncle got to his feet, and supported by the crutches, he took a few tentative steps across the flagstone floor of the croft.

"Ye see, Father. Ye can dae it," Connor said, standing to his father's side, lest he fall.

"I'm goin' to sit outside. I've seen enough of these four walls to last me a lifetime. Open the door for me, Connor," he said, and Connor hurried to do so.

Hannah's mother smiled, glancing at Hannah as the two of them returned to their chopping. A pleasant breeze blew through the croft. It was a warm day, even on the heights of the moorland, and the morning passed happily, with each of the family engaged in their respective tasks.

They shared the stew for their midday meal, eaten with a loaf of bread baked in a cooking pot placed in the embers of the fire. There was honey and oatmeal, too – a gift from the professor, who would soon be returning to Edinburgh for the new term at the university.

Hannah was helping her mother clear the dirty dishes from the table, and her uncle was regaling them with a story of a stag which had led a merry chase of gentlemen over the moorland some summers previously, when the sound of horse's hooves could be heard outside.

"Visitors?" Hannah's mother said, and she went to the window and looked out.

Hannah did the same, and she was surprised to see the sight of the equerry who had visited them following her father's death.

"The equerry," Hannah said, and her mother grimaced.

"Aye, and what does he want with us now? Are we to receive more of Her Majesty's condolences, I wonder?" she asked.

The equerry knocked at the door, and Hannah's mother went to answer, ushering him inside, where he gave a curt bow and cleared his throat.

"I come with a message from His Royal Highness, Prince Albert," he said, and Hannah's family looked at one another in surprise.

"And what does His Royal Highness want with us?" Hannah's mother demanded.

"Mary, mind yer manners," Hannah's uncle hissed, as the equerry looked somewhat taken aback.

"His Royal Highness was sorry to hear of the accident which befell you, Mr. McGinn. He notes you were a loyal worker and did much to further the building of the new castle here at Balmoral. As such, His Royal Highness has instructed me to arrange a pension in your name," the equerry replied.

Hannah's uncle stared at him in surprise. The others looked at one another, and Hannah's mother raised her hands to her mouth.

"Oh, thank the good Lord," she whispered, as Hannah's uncle shook his head in astonishment.

THE CROFTER'S DAUGHTER

"I… well, tis' very generous of His Royal Highness," he said, and the equerry nodded.

"It *is* very generous, Mr. McGinn. But the Royal Family have always ensured their workers are taken good care of. His Royal Highness wished me to convey you his best wishes and assures you of his prayers for a swift recovery," he said.

"Tis' my leg. I will nae walk on it again – nae if tis' nae operated on. But there're nay surgeons in this part of the country. We couldnae afford it if there were," Hannah's uncle replied.

The equerry nodded.

"Perhaps in time. But for now, you'll receive your pension each week. It'll be enough to keep you and your family comfortable. You've still got an income from your son's work on the estate, and I'm sure your wife and sister-in-law do what they can," he said, glancing around the croft.

"We get by," Hannah's mother said.

The equerry nodded again, and after giving some further details as to the amount and duration of the pension – which was to last in perpetuity – he bid them good day. Hannah's uncle sat shaking his head. He looked astounded at what had just transpired, and Hannah knew Prince Albert's offer had been generous.

"I never expected such a thing. I thought they'd just leave me be. Tis' remarkable," he said.

"Aye, a true miracle. After all we've suffered," Hannah's aunt said, but Hannah's mother still looked sceptical.

"Ye think a few shillin' is enough for what we've suffered. Ye forget – my husband's dead," she exclaimed.

"But Mary… they did nae need to dae anythin' for us. But a pension… it means less worry for ye. For us all," Hannah's uncle replied.

"Aye, I'm it does, Brendan. But it doesnae bring back my John, does it? These children still have nay father because of the likes of

43

Prince Albert," she said, and she turned away with tears in her eyes.

Hannah went to comfort her, and Hannah's uncle and aunt looked at one another with worried expressions on their faces.

"Tis' all right, Mother," Hannah whispered, touching her mother's hand.

Her mother looked up. There were tears running down her cheeks, and she shook her head sadly.

"Nay, Hannah. Tis' nae all right. It never will be," she replied, shaking her head sadly.

* * *

BUT THE COMING days and weeks did bring with them a sense of relief. Prince Albert was true to his word, and Hannah's uncle began to receive a small pension at the expense of the Balmoral estate. It was the equivalent of a builder's wage, the same as Hannah's cousin received for his labours, and enabled the family to live within the comforts of their means.

Their worries were alleviated, at least for now, even as Hannah's mother continued to blame the Royal Family for all their troubles. But summer was turning rapidly to autumn, and it would not be long before the bite of winter was on them.

The castle was rising in the glen below, and Hannah would often go and look down on its progress from the moorland path or accompany her cousin on his walk to work each morning.

"What will the castle be like when it's finished?" Hannah asked, as she walked alongside Connor through the woods one morning in late September.

"Tis' goin' to be quite spectacular. A tower at one end, and then a long wing stretchin' out – a bit like a church. At the far end, there'll be the entrance, with a covered part for carriages to draw up under. It'll be turreted, too. Tis' a remarkable lookin' place already," Connor replied, smiling at Hannah, who tried to imagine what the castle would be like.

Her father had often told her tales of the myths and legends of Scotland – of grand castles and brave knights, of fair ladies and charging steads. She imagined those days of adventure, picturing Balmoral as a medieval realm, where the stories her had told her could be played out.

"And will the Queen live there all the time?" she asked.

Connor shook his head.

"Nay all the time. She'll come to visit at times – in the summer, I think. But there'll always be a staff of servants there. They'll take care of the house. Perhaps ye'll get a job there. They'll be lookin' for maids in the scullery," Connor replied.

Hannah shook her head. She could only imagine what her mother would say if she was to take a job at the castle. Her mother would forbid it – however generous the salary and prospects might be.

"Ye know I cannae," she said, and Connor sighed.

"Ye cannae blame the Royal Family for what happened to yer father, Hannah. It was a terrible accident. A tragedy. But the Queen did nae push yer father into the river. He drowned because he fell. He was runnin' away from the gillies. I miss him just as ye dae. But the Royal Family – they're nae what yer mother makes them out to be. They gave me a job; they gave my father a pension. They've brought work and prospects to this remote corner of Scotland. That's worth more than a prejudice, is nae it?" he asked.

Hannah felt torn between loyalty to her mother and the obvious sense of what her cousin was saying. He was right. The Queen had not pushed her father into the river. Nor had she caused her uncle's terrible injuries to occur.

Fate had caused these things, and whilst so much had been taken, other things had been given in return. If it were not for her mother's opinion, Hannah might well have wished to take a job at the castle.

Her prospects were bleak, and even at such a tender age, she could not imagine spending her whole life on the moors, working as a crofter, and eking out pitiful existence amidst the harshness of that unforgiving landscape.

"But she will nae change her mind. She blames them for my father's death, and she'll always blame them," Hannah replied.

At that moment, a shout came from behind, and they turned to find the professor hurrying towards them. He was dressed as though for a journey, and he was leading a pony laden with bags on its back.

"Ah, Hannah, Connor, I'm glad to see ye. I called at the croft, but yer mother told me ye were away down to the castle with yer cousin. I'm leavin' for Edinburgh today. I wanted to say goodbye to ye," he said, smiling at Hannah, who had been feeling sad at the prospect of the professor leaving the moors.

She had known it was this week he was leaving, but she had hoped to have one more day together, climbing up to his croft and examining his butterfly collection for the last time.

"Oh… so soon?" she said, with a forlorn tone, and the professor nodded

"Aye, I've got to get back. I'm due to teach next week, and I've still several lectures to write and my research here to catalogue," he said, putting his hand on her shoulder and smiling at her.

"But ye'll be back, will nae, ye?" she asked, and the professor nodded again.

"Aye, next summer. There's nay better place than the moors of Balmoral to find the butterflies I so want to see. Keep a looking out for them, Hannah, and next summer ye can show me the places ye've seen them. Come now, I need to get to the railway station at Ballater. Walk with me, I'll take the road from Balmoral," he said.

They walked on down the hill, through the woods, towards

the castle. There was a chill in the air. Autumn had arrived, and it would not be long before the first snows came.

The castle, magnificent, even though unfinished, rose before them, and Hannah bid her cousin goodbye, promising to return later to walk home with him. The professor smiled at her.

"I'll miss ye," Hannah said, slipping her hand into his.

"Ye are a remarkable child, Hannah. I'm glad we've got to know one another better this summer gone. I've a present for ye," he said, and turned to rummage in the pony's saddlebag.

From it, he pulled out a small box, which he handed to Hannah, bidding her open it. She did so, and it revealed a beautiful butterfly, black and orange, perfectly preserved. She had never seen one like it, and she looked up at the professor in astonishment.

"For me?" she asked, and he nodded.

"The silver washed fritillary. Argynnis paphia, to give it is Latin name. They're not found in Scotland, though they're common in the southern part of England. I thought you'd like it as a reminder of your old friend – at least until next year," he said.

Hannah smiled at him. It was a wonderful gift; one she would surely treasure as the years went by.

"Thank you, Professor Lochray, I'll keep it safe, I promise," she said, and the professor smiled.

"I'll see you next year, Hannah, and always remember – you've got a friend in me," he said, as he waved to her cheerily and led his pony towards the Ballater road, humming to himself as he went.

Hannah looked down at the butterfly, perfectly preserved in the velvet lined box. She would keep it safe and look at it whenever she felt sad or lonely. She closed the box, glancing to find the professor gone.

He had disappeared into the trees, and Hannah was left alone. As she walked back through the woodland and up the moorland path towards home, she thought of all that had happened in the year gone by – the loss of her father, the accident involving her uncle, the kindness on the Royal Family in the face of tragedy.

"It'll all be all right, I think," she told herself, even as there was still so much uncertainty in what was to come.

She thought of the butterflies – how so much beauty could emerge from something which seemed so insignificant, ugly, even. She paused as she came to the croft, knowing her mother would have a dozen chores for her to do, and opened the box to look at the butterfly once again.

It was beautiful, and despite her troubles, Hannah vowed to look for that beauty wherever she could find it and do her best to make her father proud.

PART II

AN ACCIDENTAL ENCOUNTER

Spring 1853

Hannah was twelve years old. The years had gone by slowly but surely, just like the building of the castle, which now stood magnificently resplendent in the glen below the croft.

Life was hard without her father, and the family continued to eke out its existence on the lonely moorland above Balmoral. Hannah and her two sisters, Maeve and Caitlin, did their best to help their mother, whilst their uncle lived on his pension from Prince Albert, and Connor now worked in the stables at the "big house," where he hoped one day to become a groom.

Hannah's mother and her aunt took in mending, and Hannah had been learning all she could to help.

"Ye've stitched it the wrong way, Hannah. Never mind, just unpick it, and start again. That's the beauty of sewin'–Ye can always unpick and start again," Hannah's mother said, leaning over to examine a hem which Hannah had just stitched.

"I'm sorry, Mother. I was tryin' my best," Hannah said, feeling frustrated with herself at not having been able to do it properly, as her mother had shown her.

Her mother smiled and patted her arm.

"Practice, Hannah, that's what it takes. Practice, practice, and more practice," she said, as Hannah took up her needle and thread and tried once again.

She managed this time, and the hem of the pair of trousers was sewn straight. A pile of mending needed to be delivered to a farmhouse some miles across the moorland. Hannah was given the task of taking it in the handcart, which she would pull along the bridleway leading over the heathers.

"If I leave now, I'll be back before it gets dark," Hannah said as they finished the mending.

"Aye, go now, and we'll have yer dinner ready for ye when ye get home," her aunt said.

It was a bright spring day, with a fresh breeze blowing across the moorland, bringing with it the scent of woodland below, slowly coming back to life after the harsh winter they had endured. The snows had been thick, and Hannah and her family had spent long nights huddled in the croft by the fire.

But the arrival of spring brought with it the hope of new life, and there was a sense of expectation in the air as Hannah pulled the handcart along the bridleway, humming to herself as she went.

"Ti's a beautiful day," she thought to herself, pausing to look out over the moorland towards the castle down below.

It stood proud and magnificent amidst the pine trees, the arc of the river bending around it, and a flag–the royal standard– fluttering from the tallest tower. The appearance of the standard meant the monarch was in residence, and Hannah wondered what the Queen was like.

She had not seen her before, though Connor had told her she often came to the stables to see her favourite ponies or ride out in a horse and trap.

Hannah smiled to herself–their worlds were but a few miles apart, but they could not have been more different. In the castle, the Royal Family lived in opulence, whilst Hannah and her family lived in two rooms, high on the moorland, making ends meet as best they could. It was a remarkable contrast, one which Hannah often thought about.

"But I've got mendin' to deliver," she told herself, knowing she could not idle the day away gazing at the views across the moorland.

The farmer–Mr. McSween–lived in an isolated farmhouse some miles across the moor. He was a sheep farmer and had never married. He and Hannah's mother were friends–as much as Mr. McSween could be said to have friends–and she mended his clothes once a month, for they were always getting torn and ripped by the heathers and bracken he waded through in search of lost sheep.

The farmhouse stood out starkly against the moorland, its walls built of great rocks hewn from the mountainsides, worn, and weathered by the wind and rain that so often battered the landscape.

"Ah, Hannah, ye've come from yer mother, have ye? Bringin' my mendin' with ye?" Mr. McSween said, when he opened the farmhouse door to Hannah a short while later.

He was a tall man with an unkempt beard and long hair, his weather beaten faced was dark and lined, but his eyes were bright, and he had a keen smile on his face, a clay tobacco pipe protruding from one side of his mouth. Hannah smiled at him and nodded.

"Aye, Mr. McSween. I've brought yer mendin' for ye. Mother says it's a shillin' and sixpence," Hannah said.

The farmer rummaged in his pocket and brought out the payment, along with an extra penny, which he gave to Hannah with a wink.

"A little somethin' for ye, too, Hannah. Tis' a long walk across the moorland to my lonely farmhouse," he said, and he patted Hannah on the head.

"I like the walk, tis' a beautiful day," she said, and the farmer nodded.

"Aye, tis a beautiful day. I need to round the sheep up. They're runnin' far and wide across the moorland. But dae ye know, I saw a strange sight earlier pass by," he said, and Hannah looked at him curiously.

She had seen nothing between her mother's croft and the farm, and now she glanced around her, curious as to what Mr. McSween could mean.

"What did ye see?" she asked, and the farmer laughed.

"I saw a woman ridin' a pony–finely dressed she was, and with her nose stuck in the air, accompanyin' a boy, nae much older than ye. He was dressed like a gentleman, and they were walkin' all high and mighty past my farm. Well, tis' my land this–tis' nothin' to dae with the royal estate. I could've chased them for tresppasin'–just like yer poor father was," he said, shaking his head.

Hannah smiled. She liked Mr. McSween–he was not one to hold back on his forthright views, especially when it came to the monarchy, whom he considered foreign invaders.

"I'm sure they meant nay harm," she said, and the farmer laughed.

"Aye, that's what they'd say, too," he said, tapping his nose.

He bid Hannah goodbye, and she took up the empty handcart and began to wheel it back along the bridleway across the moor.

There was no sign of anyone on the path ahead, but the way was rough and rocky, and clung to the edge of a scree at one point, the way ahead blocked from view by a bend around a rocky outcrop. It could be treacherous for horses, and as Hannah approached, she heard a cry for help.

"Someone help! Please, anyone?" came the cry–it was a boy's voice, and dropping the handcart, Hannah rushed towards the bend in the path, coming across a terrible scene as she rounded the rocky outcrop.

It was the same boy whom Mr. McSween had described. He was standing at the edge of the path, where the scree gave way, crying out for help.

Down below, the woman–presumably his governess–was lying on the scree, her pony scrabbling on the rocks below. The pony must have lost its footing on the path, and Hannah hurried towards them, as the boy let out another cry.

"It's all right. I'll help you," Hannah called out.

She had often heard her uncle and cousin talk about the dangers of this part of the moorland path. Many a horse and rider had fallen foul of the scree, and it would take a rope and several strong men to haul the pony back up.

The boy turned to stare at her. His face was streaked with tears, and he pointed down to where the woman was clinging on below.

"We've got to help her–my Mimi," he exclaimed.

"I'll run and fetch Mr. McSween. He'll be able to help her," Hannah said, and before the boy could reply, she had darted back along the path, making in the direction of the farmhouse.

Hannah was used to running across the moors. She was fast and agile, and it was not long before she was knocking frantically at the door of the farmhouse, calling out for McSween, and praying he had not already set off in pursuit of his sheep.

"What's all this? What's wrong?" he exclaimed, pulling open the door and staring at Hannah in amazement.

"It's the woman and the boy, Mr. McSween. Her pony slipped on the scree. She fell. Ye've got to help her, please. I'll run and fetch Connor, too," Hannah said.

For all the farmer's disparaging remarks about the boy and his governess, he wasted no time in responding, and the two of them were soon hurrying back towards the sight of the accident.

The governess was still clinging to the scree, though she was in no danger of falling. It was not a sheer drop, more a slippery incline, which proved hard to maintain one's footing on.

The farmer had brought a rope, and with Hannah and the boy's help, they secured it to a gnarled tree growing out of the rocks.

"I'll go down, she'll be all right," the farmer said, and carefully choosing his footing, he descended the scree.

Hannah was left alone with the boy, whom she now recognised as the same she had seen accompanying his uncle, the Duke of Braemar, on his inspection of the works on the castle several years ago.

"Yer the duke's nephew, are nae ye?" she asked.

The boy nodded.

"That's right. I've come to stay in Balmoral. The Queen's my Godmother. Mimi and I were just out for a walk with the pony," he said, peering fearfully over the edge of the scree, to where Mr. McSween was now helping the governess climb back up.

The terror of what had happened appeared to have taken away some of the boy's arrogance, and Hannah could only feel sorry for him for having witnessed such a traumatic incident.

"It'll be all right. Mr. McSween has her now," Hannah said.

The boy nodded.

"When she fell, she screamed. I didn't know what to do. There was no one around. These moors are so lonely, and we're miles from the castle. If you hadn't come along…" he said, his words trailing off into the awful possibility of what might have happened.

Hannah smiled at him.

"But I did come along, and we're helpin' Mimi, now. Why dae ye call her that?" Hannah asked, for surely Mimi was not the governess' real name.

"Her real name's Miriam. But when I was a child, I couldn't say Miriam, so I said Mimi, and the name's stuck," he replied, looking slightly embarrassed, as Hannah laughed.

"And what's yer name?" she asked, realising she only knew the boy by sight, and not by name.

He was the nephew of the Duke of Braemar, but that was all Hannah knew of him, and she was curious to learn more.

"My name's Hamish, Hamish Alexander Beaufort Williams," he said, and again, Hannah laughed.

"I'll just call ye Hamish. I'm Hannah. Just Hannah. Hannah McGinn," Hannah replied, holding out her hand to the boy, who took and gave a weak smile.

"There's a McGinn working in the castle stables. I spoke to him the other day. He fetched a saddle for me," he said, and Hannah nodded.

"That's my cousin, Connor," she replied.

A shout now came from below, and Hannah looked down the scree to see Mr. McSween struggling to help the governess. She was having an attack of hysterics and refusing to go any further.

"Hannah, go and fetch yer mother, and anyone else ye can find. Tell them to bring more ropes. I'll stay here. She will nae move any further. She needs a woman to coax her up," Mr. McSween called up.

"Mimi, you'll be all right, we'll fetch more help," Hamish called down, and the governess looked fearfully from below.

Her dress was torn, and her face and hands were muddy. She looked nothing like the elegant lady whom Mr. McSween had described, and Hannah was reminded of the fact there was little difference between those in grand positions and the lowliest of the low when it came to tragedy.

"Come along, run with me. We'll go to my mother's croft. Connor will be back from work now, and he can come to help," Hannah said, beckoning Hamish to follow her.

The two of them ran off along the moorland path, and Hannah was surprised at the ease with which Hamish kept up with her.

"You run at quite a pace," he said, as they approached the croft.

"I'm used to it. I've always run across the moorland, ever since I was a child," she replied.

Her mother was standing outside the croft, beating the dust from the hearthside rug, and she looked up in surprised as Hannah and Hamish approached.

"Hannah, what's all this?" she asked, staring at her in astonishment.

"It's Mimi, Mother, I mean… Hamish's governess. She fell down the scree. Mr. McSween is there, he says to send help. She will nae climb any further. She's in hysterics," Hannah said.

Her mother looked from her to Hamish, her eyes narrowing. Hannah knew what she was thinking, but at that moment, Connor emerged from the croft, staring at Hamish in disbelief.

"My Lord," he said, giving a curt bow.

"There's nay time, Connor. Quickly. Ye've got to come. Bring a rope. It's Hamish's governess, she's fallen down the scree–the pony, too. Mr. McSween says for us all to come–she needs a woman to coax up her up, Mother," Hannah said, imploring her mother with a desperate tone.

Hannah's aunt and sisters had emerged from the croft now, her uncle resting inside, and the story was recounted for a third time. But Connor had already seized a coil of rope and pulled on his boots.

"We'll help her. Come along," he said, running off along the moorland path, closely followed by Hamish.

Hannah gave her mother an imploring look. She knew she had no desire to help those whom she still held responsible for her husband's death, but they could not leave the governess–and Mr. McSween–to her fate.

"Ye watch the two children, Rose. We'll nae be long," Hannah's mother said, and to Hannah's relief, she hurried after Connor and Hamish, calling for Hannah to follow her.

It did not take long for them to reach the scree. Mr. McSween and the governess were still some distance down, and whilst the governess was no longer in hysterics, she had not moved any further up the rock face. Connor tied his rope to the same tree to which Mr. McSween's was attached and gently edged down from the path.

"She won't move," Hamish said, as Hannah's mother rolled her eyes.

"What does she expect? She needs to put one foot in the front of the other," she said, rolling up her sleeves.

"Mother, be careful," Hannah said, but her mother–who had always been fearless–now took hold of the same rope Connor was descending on and edged down from the path.

Hannah watched fearfully as her mother and Connor reached the governess. She could not hear what was being said, but the governess now moved forward, clinging to the scree as Connor and Mr. McSween guarded her flank to prevent her from falling backwards.

"I'm ever so grateful to you all," Hamish said, as he and Hannah stood at the top of the scree, watching the rescue.

"Ye'd dae the same for us," Hannah replied, even as the thought of her father flashed through her mind.

"I suppose you rather resent us, don't you?" he said, and Hannah turned to him with a curious expression on her face.

"I daenae know what ye mean," she replied, even as what he said had a ring of truth to it.

He sighed and shook his head, glancing down the scree, where the governess was being coaxed bit by bit towards the path by Hannah's mother.

"The building of Balmoral, the estate cutting through lands that were once the realm of those who farmed them. People like Mimi and I causing you such inconvenience," he replied.

Hannah smiled and shrugged. She was beginning to change her mind about the Royal Family. Connor was right. There was nothing to be gained by blaming them for an accident.

But Hannah knew her mother did not feel the same. She

would carry her resentment to the grave, and an incident like this would only serve to reinforce her opinions.

"Some dae, aye. They see the likes of ye as incomers, with nae right to be here. I daenae know. We live as best we can. Yer family–the Royal Family–they've been kind to us. When my father died, the Queen sent us a gift, and when my uncle had his accident, Prince Albert gave him a pension to live by. Yer family gave my cousin a job, and in time, perhaps my sisters will come to work at the house, too. I daenae resent ye," she replied, and Hamish nodded.

"I'm sorry–your father, he died?" he asked, and Hannah nodded.

"He was poachin' in the river by the castle – tis' some years ago now, before the new house was built. He was caught and ran away. He fell into the river and drowned," she said, shaking her head.

Hamish looked at her sadly.

"My parents died, too. That's why I go from grand house to grand house, fostered on which ever distant relative might have me for a few weeks here, or a month there. My uncle's been very good to me, and my godmother lets me stay here as much as I wish. I think they feel guilty, you see," he said, and now it was Hannah's turn to be confused.

She felt sorry for him. She knew the pain of losing one parent, but to lose both was a tragedy.

"I'm sorry. It must be awful for ye. I could nae imagine life without my mother," she said, and Hamish nodded.

"It's not easy. My parents were killed in India. My father was an official there–sent by his great aunt, the Queen. There was an uprising and violence. I was caught up in it, too, but I escaped with Mimi. My parents were killed, and we returned to England shortly afterwards," he said, shaking his head.

Hannah's heart went out to him. She knew just how he must have felt, even as his own pain was surely far greater than hers.

"I'm so sorry, I can't imagine what ye must have gone through," she said, and Hamish shook his head.

"It's... hard," he replied.

Hannah was about to ask another question–there was so much she wanted to know–when a shout from below caused them both to look up. The governess had reached a point just below the path, and Mr. McSween and Connor were helping her over the final rough ground, as Hannah's mother continued to encourage her.

"That's it, lass. Just a few steps more. Ye've done so well," Hannah's mother said.

Hannah knew how difficult this encounter must have been for her mother. Hamish and Mimi represented everything for which Hannah's mother blamed the Royal Family. But despite this, Hannah knew her to be kind and compassionate in abundance, and if a person was in need, Hannah's mother would be the one to help.

"Oh, thank you. I was so frightened. I couldn't move. Poor Mr. McSween was trying his best, but if it weren't for you, Mrs. McGinn, I don't think I'd have made it. Oh, the poor pony, it's still down there. What can we do, Connor?" the governess exclaimed.

Behind the mud and torn dress, she was a pretty woman, perhaps only twenty years old, and now Hamish hurried to embrace her as she climbed up onto the path and to safety.

"Oh, Mimi, I was so worried," Hamish exclaimed.

"I'll go down to the stables and bring a couple of the grooms up here. We can get the pony, daenae worry," he said, smiling at the governess, for whom it appeared he had something of an affection.

The pony itself was grazing happily at the bottom of the scree, though it could not remain there forever, and Connor hurried off along the moorland path in the direction of the croft and the castle.

"Sit down here for a moment, lass. Catch yer breath," Hannah's mother said, helping the governess to a rock by the edge of the path.

She sat down, and Hamish sat next to her, putting his arm around her and kissing her on the cheek. The affection between them was clear, and Hannah could only imagine what they had faced together in India.

"I was so worried, Mimi, but Hannah was the one who saved us. She came along as I was calling for help. It was her who went back to fetch Mr. McSween, and then the two of us ran to her mother's croft to fetch the others," Hamish said.

The governess looked up at Hannah and smiled. She had a pretty smile, and Hannah smiled back at her.

"Then we owe you all a debt of gratitude. Thank you," she said.

"The scree can be treacherous—even for experienced riders," Mr. McSween said, shaking his head.

He pulled out a handkerchief and mopped his brow. He was covered in mud and dust, as was Hannah's mother, who now invited them back to the croft for refreshment.

"Connor can bring the grooms up for the pony. He'll know to send someone to fetch ye," she said, and the governess once again thanked her for her kindness.

"I'm sure we don't deserve it at all," she said, as Hannah's mother took her by the arm and led her towards the croft.

Mr. McSween had excused himself, telling them he had had sheep to round up, and Hannah and Hamish followed behind, walking side by side.

"Yer close to yer governess, I see," Hannah said, and Hamish nodded.

"We've been through a lot. We had to flee in the middle of the night, then take a boat all the way to England. Seeing her on the scree brought back memories of the danger. Anyway, she's safe now. That's all that matters," Hamish said.

Hannah nodded. There was a great deal she wanted to ask him. They came from such different worlds, but if the incident on the scree had proved one thing, it was that people are not so different when it comes to facing danger and difficulty. Rich or poor, it makes no difference when life is threatened, and help is required.

"Aye, she's safe," Hannah replied, as the two of them followed Hannah's mother and the governess towards the crofts.

THE DUKE OF BRAEMAR

"Sit yerselves down, we'll make some tea," Hannah's mother said, as they entered the croft a short while later.

"You mustn't go to any trouble on our account, Mrs. McGinn," the governess said, but Hannah's mother ignored her and began fussing around the fire with a kettle.

Hannah's aunt pulled out two chairs for the governess and Hamish to sit in, whilst Hannah's two sisters peered curiously out from behind the bed curtains, as Hannah's uncle sat up in bed, peering curiously at them.

"Tis' all right, ye can come out," Hannah said, beckoning Maeve and Caitlin towards her.

Her sisters stepped shyly forward, and the governess smiled at them.

"Aren't you both the prettiest little things? What delightful children, Mrs. McGinn," she said, and Hannah's mother turned to her and smiled.

"Well, I try to raise them right. Tis' difficult without their father here," she said.

The governess looked startled at this revelation and apologised.

"Oh, you're a widow? It must be so hard for you," she said, shaking her head.

"Aye, my husband died some years ago. An accident in the river. He was… fishin' for salmon, and fell in," she said.

Hannah was surprised. Usually, her mother would tell anyone who would listen to the story of how her husband was killed by the actions of the Royal Family, but it seemed she had no desire to upset the governess and poured the tea without further comment.

"How terrible. But we know what that's like, too, don't we, Hamish? Poor Hamish lost both his parents in India," the governess said, and Hannah's mother looked up with genuine sorrow on her face.

"Is that so? I'm sorry to hear that," she said, and Hamish nodded.

"It's very kind of you to say so. Hannah and I were talking… it seems we have that much in common, at least," he said.

"Aye, tis' a tragedy for a child to lose their parent. Rich or poor, it makes nay difference. Tis' love that matters, and when a child is deprived of that love… aye, tis' terrible," Hannah's mother replied, shaking her head sadly.

The last piece of a fruitcake, given to Connor as Christmas present by the estate, was cut into small pieces and served, and it seemed the governess was greatly revived by the tea.

She told them about her and Hamish's adventures in India, and how they came to England at the behest of Hamish's uncle, the Duke of Braemar.

"It hasn't been easy, has it, Hamish? But we've managed. As you say, Mrs. McGinn–it's love that matters. If a child knows they're loved, what more does it need?" she replied.

On this, Hannah's mother could not disagree, and she poured

the governess another cup of tea, and offered her the last of the fruitcake. Hannah glanced at Hamish and smiled. He was no longer the haughty-looking boy who had seemed so distant when she had first seen him touring the building works with his uncle. They were not so different–separated by wealth, but much the same when it came to the things they had endured.

"Will ye stay long at Balmoral, Master Hamish?" Hannah's mother asked, but before Hamish could reply, the sound of horse's hooves caused them all to look up.

Outside, half a dozen horses had just ridden up to the croft, and a moment later there came a knocking at the door. Hannah's mother went to answer it, and Hannah was amazed to see the Duke of Braemar himself standing in the doorway.

"My good woman, I understand you've done me a great service this day," he said, removing his top hat, as Hannah's mother stepped back to allow him to enter.

"Uncle, we've so much to tell you. There was a terrible accident. Mimi's pony fell down the scree. But Hannah came, and she went to fetch Mr. McSween, and then Mrs. McGinn, and Connor. They all helped us, Uncle," Hamish exclaimed, as the governess rose to her feet and curtsied.

Hannah did the same, though she was not used to doing so, and her sisters copied her, along with her aunt. The duke was a handsome man, elderly, but with a keen face and bright eyes. He was wearing riding clothes–a frock-coat, breeches, and high boots. Outside, the men who had accompanied him–gentlemen of the royal household, Hannah presumed–stood waiting.

"Connor came to me at once and told me. We do owe you– and the good Mr. McSween–a debt of gratitude, madam," the duke said, turning to Hannah's mother, who blushed.

"Tis' only what anyone would have done in our place. I'm glad there was nay tragedy involved. From what I've learned, it seems both these children have suffered enough," she said, glancing at Hannah and Hamish, who were standing side by side.

"Ah, yes… your poor husband. I know the story, Mrs. McGinn. As for my nephew, you're right, he's known that same loss, and I'm only glad I don't have to share that loss today. He and Mimi are family to me," he said, and reaching into his pocket, he took out a purse of coins, from which he counted five gold sovereigns.

"Tis' too much, sir," Hannah's mother exclaimed, for such a sum represented more money than they had ever seen.

"One for you, madam. One for Mr. McSween. One for Connor. One for Hannah, and one for the lady and her husband who minded the children whilst you were away at your good works," the duke said, winking at Hannah's aunt, who stared at the sovereign in astonishment

"Thank ye, sir," she said, shaking her head, and turning to Hannah's uncle, who had grown quite pale.

"Come now, Hamish. We shan't keep these good people from their work any longer. We've cost them enough of their valuable time. Are you all right, Mimi? Can you walk?" the duke asked, and the governess nodded.

"I'm quite all right, your grace. Mrs. McGinn's ministrations have restored me to full health after my shock," she replied, and she took Hannah's mother's hand in hers and smiled.

Hannah watched, curious as to the look on her mother's face. There was a thawing there, as though the anger of those past years was lessening. She nodded and smiled in return.

"I'm glad yer all right, lass," she said, and the governess kissed her on the cheek.

"I won't forget you," the governess said.

Hannah glanced at Hamish, wondering if they would meet again. Their two worlds existed side by side, though never meeting. But for a few brief hours, they had shared one another's worlds, and Hannah would be sad to say goodbye.

"I've sent some men with Connor to retrieve the pony. Thank

Mr. McSween on my behalf. I really am very grateful to you all," the duke said, beckoning Hamish to follow him.

But before he did so, Hamish cleared his throat and glanced at Hannah with a smile on his face.

"Uncle, do you think Hannah might come to Balmoral sometimes? Or I might come here?" he asked.

His uncle looked at him in surprise, but nodded in agreement.

"I don't see why not. The Queen returns to London on Friday. You could invite Hannah to tea after that. Say on Sunday afternoon," he said, and Hamish smiled, turning to Hannah, who could hardly believe what was being suggested.

"Would you like to come for tea at the castle?" he asked.

Hannah glanced at her mother. Would she allow her to do so? But her mother nodded and made no protest against the idea.

"I'd like that, aye," she said, and Hamish grinned.

"Excellent. Sunday afternoon then. Come at two O'clock. I can show you the house, and then we'll have tea," he said, and bidding the others farewell, the party left the croft.

As the door closed, Hannah's mother breathed a deep sigh and shook her head. Hannah's uncle was staring at the gold sovereign her aunt had handed him, whilst Maeve and Caitlin looked up in amazement at Hannah, who could hardly believe what had happened.

"Am I really to take tea at the castle, Mother?" Hannah asked, and her mother nodded.

"Aye, it seems so, Hannah. Which means we've got a lot to dae," she replied, shaking her head.

* * *

"Hold still, Hannah. I cannae tie yer hair properly if ye keep movin' around all the time," Hannah's mother exclaimed.

It was Sunday afternoon, and Hannah had spent the day, following the morning's church service, preparing to take tea at

Balmoral. Her mother had insisted on her taking a bath in the copper tub, and her aunt had heated water, whilst her mother had scrubbed her from head to toe.

She was wearing a freshly laundered dress, and had a new bonnet to wear, which her aunt had decorated with silk flowers.

"I'm holdin' still, Mother," she said, as her mother ran a brush vigorously through her hair.

"There now, ye look pretty, Hannah. Turn around and let me look at ye," her mother said, and Hannah dutifully obeyed.

Her mother licked the end of her thumb and smudged Hannah's nose, smiling at her and nodding.

"Aye, ye dae look pretty, Hannah," she said.

Maeve and Caitlin were watching from the rug on the hearth, and Hannah smiled at them, offering them both a hand.

"Will ye both walk with me to the castle?" she asked, as her aunt put the bonnet on Hannah's head.

Her two sisters nodded, and Hannah was now ready to leave. Her mother inspected her for a final time, before pronouncing her ready to leave.

"But daenae come back filled with airs and graces. There'll be nay silver tea service and bone china come dinner time," she said, smiling at Hannah, who laughed.

"It's only tea, Mother," she replied, even as she felt nervous at the prospect of what was to come.

She had never been inside the house before. Balmoral was another world—one she could only dream of. Connor had told her a little–how she had to behave, speaking only when spoken to, and showing deference even to the servants.

"There's a hierarchy, Hannah. We're at the bottom, and everyone else is above us," he had told her.

But despite her nerves, Hannah was looking forward to seeing Hamish once again, and now, hand in hand with Maeve and Caitlin, she set off for the castle.

"What will ye say to him? Are ye nervous?" Maeve asked, as they made their way along the moorland path.

"Aye, but tis' Hamish who's invited me. I'm sure he'll make me welcome," Hannah replied.

When they came in sight of the castle, Hannah sent her two sisters home. They wanted to come with her to the door, but she forbade them, promising she would tell them all about it when she returned.

"Will ye bring us a piece of cake? Or a scone?" Caitlin asked, and Hannah laughed.

"I cannae take the food, can I?" she said, shaking her head.

Her sisters turned reluctantly back along the moorland path, and Hannah made her way down through the woods towards the castle.

Her heart was beating fast, and now she even began to wonder if it had all been a dream – had Hamish really invited her to take tea with him? The castle looked imposing as Hannah walked nervously up the driveway.

She had not asked where Hamish would meet her, knowing only she was due there at two O'clock, and the clock on the tower above the doorway said one minute to. Taking a deep breath, Hannah went up to the door and rang the bell, which sounded deep in the depths of the house.

Footsteps approached, and an imperious-looking man dressed in black, who peered at Hannah over a pair of half-moon spectacles, opened the door.

"Yes?" he asked, looking Hannah up and down with a disdainful look.

"Please, I'm here to…" she began, but before she could finish speaking, a voice behind the man called out.

"Hannah, you're here. Let her in, Wigmore. She's my guest. This is the girl who saved Mimi," Hamish said, appearing behind the man, who turned to look at him in surprise.

"My Lord, I didn't realise..." he said, looking somewhat bemused.

"Come in, Hannah," Hamish said, beckoning Hannah inside.

Hannah did as she was told, entering a grand hallway decorated with paintings and all manner of objects and furniture. She had never seen such a place and stared around her in amazement.

"I wasnae sure where to come," she said, taking off her bonnet.

The man–whom she assumed was the butler–took the bonnet from her and gave a curt bow.

"You came to the right door. You're a guest. Only servants go to the kitchen door," Hamish said, smiling at her.

He was dressed in a tartan kilt, with sporran and long white socks, a white shirt, and jacket–appearing every bit the Scottish laird.

"I've always wondered what tis' like in here," Hannah said, still gazing around her in awe.

A wide staircase led up to a gallery above, where suits of armour lined a carpeted landing, and further portraits adorned the walls. At the centre of the hallways stood a large table, where a vase of heather and spring blooms stood in the middle.

The floor was covered in a rug, and a fire blazed in the hearth. It was magnificent, and Hamish now led Hannah through into the state rooms, pointing out objects as they went.

"Prince Albert brought these back from Africa. Aren't they magnificent?" Hamish said, pointing to a set of tribal masks displayed in a drawing room decorated in an oriental style.

"I can hardly believe it. And ye can live here if ye wish?" Hannah asked, marvelling at the sight of a magnificent painting showing the wedding of Queen Victoria to Prince Albert.

"My godmother usually comes here in the summer. But my uncle has an estate at Braemar, too. I'm to stay here during the winter, and when the Queen returns, I'll go to my uncle's estate – or stay here. It's not been decided yet," he said, as now they came to a small sitting room at the end of the house, where a magnificent tea had been laid out for them.

Hannah had never seen so much food in one place. There were four stands, each laden with dainty cakes, delicately made sandwiches, tiny scones, and all manner of other treats. It was enough to feed twenty, let alone two, and Hannah stared at the tea table in amazement.

"Good day, Hannah, how nice of you to join us," Mimi said, rising from a chair by the window to greet them.

Hannah smiled and bobbed into an awkward curtsey, which made Hamish laugh.

"You don't need to curtsey to Mimi. You probably should've curtsied to me. But I don't mind. We're friends. We rescued Mimi together, and that means you don't have to curtsey to me," he said.

Hannah smiled nervously, but the governess laughed and shook her head.

"Master Hamish likes his little jokes, don't you?" she said, as they sat down at the tea table.

"But are you… a Lord?" Hannah asked, for she really felt quite confused as to how she should address her new friend.

"My full title is Lord Hamish Alexander Beaufort Williams, Viscount Draycott," Hamish said, smiling at Hannah, as Mimi poured the tea.

"I've never taken tea with a Lord before," Hannah said, wondering if it might be possible to take some of the delicious-looking food home for the rest of her family.

"I shouldn't think you have, no. But I'm pleased you are. I've got no one to play with here. I had lots of friends back in India, didn't I, Mimi? But since I've come to England, I've had no one to play with," he said, looking somewhat forlorn.

Once again, Hannah realised there was little difference between them. A rich boy could be a friendless boy, just as a poor girl could have dozens of friends.

But friendship mattered. It could not be bought, and Hannah felt sorry for Hamish, even as she herself had few friends, either. Her sisters were her friends, and there was the professor and Mr. McSween. But as for companions of her own age, Hannah had none.

"I don't have many friends, either," she replied, and Hamish smiled at her.

"Then we can be friends, can't we? We're already friends," he said, helping himself to a sandwich.

Hannah was unsure as to the etiquette of how much she might help herself to. But for everything she ate, Mimi offered her something more, and it was not long before they had made a significant inroad to the four cake stands.

"I've never eaten such delicious food," she said, dabbing her mouth with a napkin.

Her mother would not believe her eyes if she saw Hannah now, and Hannah felt guilty for enjoying such opulence, when her family subsisted mainly on soup and bread.

"You should take some home for your family, Hannah. I'm sure your sisters would like to try a cake or two," Mimi said, and Hannah nodded.

"Thank ye, they would," Hannah replied.

"I should come and take tea with you. You can show me the moorland. I never know where to go on my walks. Do you see wildlife? My uncle says there're magnificent stags, eagles, even big cats up there," Hamish said, getting down from the table and bringing over a picture book, which he proceeded to open and examine, showing Hannah pictures of the animals he was referring to.

"Now, Master Hamish. You mustn't invite yourself for tea. You've got to remember, not everyone has the means we have," Mimi said, but Hannah shook her head.

"I'd like that, but it would only be bread and drippin'–or griddle cakes with jam," she said.

Hamish looked at her in delight and nodded.

"That's marvellous. I'd love to. When can I come? I'm so bored here. Won't you let me, Mimi? Please?" he implored.

"I can ask my mother and then send word with Connor," Hannah replied.

She liked the idea of inviting Hamish to tea. Despite their vast separation, they had found much in common whilst taking tea together–a shared love of wildlife in particular.

Hamish had told Hannah of his disdain for the hunting which took place on the estate, a disdain which Hannah shared, and when the time came for them to depart, she was sad to say goodbye.

"I'll see you very soon. Send word with Connor as soon as you can," Hamish said as he walked with Hannah to the hallway.

The governess had seen to it the remnants of the tea were boxed up for Hannah to take home with her, and she handed the boxes to Hannah at the door.

"I hope your sisters enjoy the cakes," Mimi said, as she and Hamish bid Hannah goodbye.

"I know they will. Thank ye," Hannah said, and no longer feeling nervous at all, she left Balmoral through the front door, walking happily through the woods and onto the moorland path.

The rest of the family were amazed to hear her tales of the afternoon, and when she opened the boxes, they marvelled at the sight of the delicious cakes, sandwiches, and scones.

"I've never tasted anything so delicious," Maeve exclaimed, and the others expressed similar sentiments.

"Mother, might Hamish come here for tea next week?" Hannah asked after they had finished eating.

She feared what her mother might say, but to her surprise, she nodded and smiled at Hannah, shaking her head.

"I did nae want ye to get airs and graces, Hannah. But I'm glad ye've found a friend in Hamish–albeit a strange one. Aye, he can come for tea. But it'll be bread and drippin'–nothin' fancy," she replied, and Hannah smiled.

She *had* found a friend in Hamish, and she was only too glad to think of that friendship developing, as strange as it seemed. Their lives were worlds apart, but they had much in common, too, and Hannah felt certain they would find much more if only that friendship continued.

THE MONARCH OF THE GLEN

"Daenae touch that, Caitlin, tis' for Hamish," Hannah said, turning around to find her youngest sister helping herself to a slice of bread and dripping from a plate on the middle of the table, which had been laid for tea.

Caitlin looked up at her sulkily and pouted.

"But I want some," she said, and Hannah sighed.

"Ye can have some when Hamish arrives. He will nae be long," she said, as her mother set a plate of griddle cakes on the table, along with a pot of jam.

"There, now, tis' nae a cake stand at Balmoral, but it'll dae," she said.

The kettle was whistling over the fire, and Hannah had spent the morning preparing for Hamish's arrival. He was due at two O'clock, and they would take tea before walking out over the moor in search of the stags.

Hannah had seen one the previous day. A magnificent creature, standing proudly on a rocky outcrop between the croft and Mr. McSween's farmhouse. She knew the poor creature was in danger–there was to be a stalk from Balmoral, and the hunters would be searching for a worthy trophy to take down.

"Thank ye, Mother. I know ye daenae really want Hamish here," Hannah said, but her mother shook her head.

"I've nay quarrel with the lad, Hannah. He's only a child, like ye, and I'm glad ye've made a friend in him. Tis' a lonely life for ye up here, and I daenae think tis' right for ye to always be alone," her mother replied.

Hannah smiled at her. She loved her mother dearly, and whilst life was hard for them, her mother had always strived to do what was best for Hannah and her two sisters. At that moment, a knock came at the door, and Hannah went to open it, finding Hamish and Mimi standing on the threshold.

"We're not late, are we?" Mimi asked as Hannah ushered them inside.

"Nae at all. Come in," Hannah said, smiling at Hamish, who had brought his picture book with him, and grinned back at her.

"Ah, Mrs. McGinn. How good to see you again," the governess said, and she greeted Hannah's mother warmly, offering her a set of embroidered handkerchiefs she had made by way of a thank you for the rescue.

"Dae sit down. Tis' nae much, but yer welcome to it," Hannah's mother said, ushering Hamish and the governess to the table.

"It looks delicious, thank you," Mimi said, as Hannah's mother served the tea.

Hamish had never eaten bread and dripping, but he devoured two large slices and declared them to be the most delicious thing he had ever eaten.

"And this jam is wonderful. It's so tart. What's it made of?" he asked, as he ate a griddle cake smothered with bright purple preserve.

"Tis' berries from the moor, Master Hamish. Hannah picked them," Hannah's mother replied, looking pleased at the compliment she had received.

"I can show ye where they grow," Hannah said, and Hamish grinned at her again.

"I'd like that. Can we go and find the stag now? I'm so excited. You don't need to come, do you, Mimi?" he said, and the governess shook her head.

"No, Hamish, I won't come. I'm sure Mrs. McGinn and I can find plenty to talk about, and I'll help her to clear up. You two go out and play," the governess replied, and Hannah and Hamish hurried out of the croft.

Maeve and Caitlin were not allowed to go, and Hannah noticed them standing glumly at the window as she and Hamish ran past. But Hannah was happy to be alone with her new friend, and now they made their way up the hill from the croft, in the direction of the professor's croft.

He was not yet returned from Edinburgh, but Hannah knew the stags often fed in the trees which bordered the professor's small holding, and to which she now led Hamish, following a path which led up the mountainside, climbing steeply from the moorland.

"I feel like a Himalayan explorer," Hamish said, grinning at Hannah as they climbed higher.

"Have ye been there? To the Himalayas, I mean?" she asked, and Hamish nodded.

"I have, yes. I've been all over India with my parents. I was born there. Some of it I remember, some of it I must ask Mimi about. It's a wonderful place. I think you'd like it," he said.

Hannah had never left the moor, let alone travelled to distant lands. She could only imagine what a place like India would be like.

"What's it like? I've never even seen a picture of it, though I've heard the professor talk about it," she said.

"The professor?" Hamish asked, as now they came in sight of the lonely croft, where Professor Lochray spent his summers.

"Aye, my friend Professor Lochray. He studies butterflies. He gave me one, once. Would ye like to see it?" Hannah asked.

She always kept the box containing the silver washed fritillary in her pocket. She liked to take it out and look at it, and now she paused, holding out the box for Hamish.

It was her most precious possession, and the fact she trusted him to see it was a sign of their deepening friendship. He opened the box, and his eyes grew wide as he gazed at the preserved butterfly inside.

"It's beautiful," he exclaimed, and Hannah smiled.

"The professor told me tis' nae to be found in Scotland, but there're parts of England where it's been sighted. I treasure it," she said, closing the box and replacing it in her pocket.

"I'm not surprised. I'd love to have something like that. You're very lucky, Hannah," he said, and Hannah smiled.

"The professor and I are good friends. Perhaps you could meet him when he comes back in the summer," she replied.

They climbed on up the mountainside, past the professor's croft and up to where the ground levelled out, and trees grew across a wide plateau. Hannah had keen eyes, and she looked around her, trying to catch a glimpse of the stags. The wind blew cold up here, and Hannah pulled her shawl tightly around her shoulders, stooping down into the heathers so she might keep out of the scent of the stags.

Hamish did the same, and now Hannah spotted one of the creatures standing at the edge of the trees. She pointed to it, signalling for Hamish to stay low.

"It's magnificent," Hamish whispered as they watched the stag emerge onto the moorland.

Hannah was not certain if she had seen the creature before. Its antlers were spectacular, and it had a glossy coat and a proud face. It lifted its head and let out a bellow, which echoed across the moorland.

"Tis' callin' for the others," Hannah whispered, and they

watched as the stag waited by the treeline for more of the stags to appear.

Some were much younger, their antlers barely formed, whilst the hinds followed behind. It was a small herd and moved cautiously out from the cover of the trees as Hannah and Hamish watched from a slightly elevated position downwind of them.

"I can't believe we're so close. I've been forced to hunt with my uncle on dozens of occasions, and we never get this close," Hamish said.

"That's because we daenae want to kill them. I've seen the huntin' parties walkin' up from Balmoral before. The herd know they're comin'–they can smell them. As soon as a gun goes off, they flee. But we're only here to watch," Hannah replied.

They watched the deer for an hour or so as they grazed on the heathers. Hamish was transfixed, and the two of them would happily have remained there all afternoon if the fear of a scolding from Mimi and Hannah's mother had not drawn them to return down the mountainside.

At last, the herd retreated into the trees, and were gone, the stag the last to return to safety, as though shepherding his flock.

"I still can't believe we got so close. My uncle's always trying to teach me how to stalk, but I'm not very good at it at all," he said, and Hannah smiled.

"Stay downwind of them. If they smell ye–or see ye–they'll run. We were downwind of them, and they did nae see us," Hannah replied.

She had always watched the wildlife on the moorlands, but especially the stags. They were magnificent creatures, and she had never understood why anyone should wish to turn them into trophies. At Balmoral, she had seen several stag's heads, triumphantly displayed as tokens of hunting prowess. But the sight of them had only saddened her, and she felt sorry for Hamish for being forced to take part in such blood sports.

"I could've watched them all day," he said, and Hannah smiled.

THE CROFTER'S DAUGHTER

"Me, too. They're remarkable creatures. The true monarchs of the glen," she said, and Hamish laughed.

"Don't let my godmother hear you saying that," he replied.

"Are ye close to the Queen?" Hannah asked, for she was curious to learn more about the Royal Family, even as they appeared distant and aloof.

"She has dozens of godchildren. But my father was a favourite of hers. She's his great aunt–was his great aunt. So, I suppose I'm related to her somehow, though I'm not sure how. She writes to me each week, and I write back to her. She asks me to take care of Balmoral for her – she means my uncle, of course. I like her. She's always been kind to me. Prince Albert can be stern, and the princesses are haughty. I don't see them much. I suppose I don't really know where I fit into it all," Hamish replied.

Once again, Hannah felt sorry for him. He lived in a gilded cage. He was an orphan, but privilege prevented him from entering the poorhouse. His family took care of him, but he really had no one, except his uncle and Mimi.

"Well, I'm glad we've met," Hannah said, and Hamish smiled at her.

"So am I," he replied, as they came in sight of the croft.

Mimi was waiting outside for them, and tutted as they approached, raising her eyebrows at Hamish, and chastising him for his tardiness.

"You've been gone for hours," she exclaimed.

"We were watching the stags, Mimi. We saw a whole herd of them. I hate to think of my uncle going up there to shoot them. Do you think we can stop him?" Hamish asked.

The governess shook her head and laughed.

"Stop a gentleman of the royal household from shooting a gun at a living creature for sport? I don't think so, Hamish. You'll never persuade your uncle not to shoot, I'm afraid. Fortunately for you, he's not a very good shot–not that I said that, of course," she replied, glancing at Hannah, and smiling.

They bid one another goodbye, and Hannah watched as Hamish and Mimi made their way along the moorland path back towards Balmoral.

"Well, Hannah–did ye enjoy bein' a lady for the day? Was bread and drippin' acceptable to ye?" her mother asked, coming to join her outside the croft.

Hannah looked up at her and smiled.

"He's nae like that," she said, looking forward to seeing Hamish again, and knowing there was far more they had in common than divided them.

A LUCKY SHOT

Hannah went to answer the door, and was surprised to find Hamish on the step, wearing tweeds, and with an excited expression on his face.

"Can you come? My uncle and the others are stalking the stag. They're having terrible trouble finding the herd. I don't want them to find them, but perhaps if you came, we could see where they were and put my uncle off the scent," he said.

Hannah had been helping her mother with the mending, and she looked around at her imploringly.

"Can I go, Mother?" she asked.

Her mother looked doubtful, glancing at her aunt, who smiled.

"Let her go, Mary. She works hard every day. Tis' a terrible thing to see the stags killed for sport. Perhaps she can prevent it," she said, and Hannah's mother nodded.

"But daenae get into trouble, Hannah. Dae ye promise me?" she said, and Hannah nodded.

She snatched up her shawl and hurried out of the croft as the cries of Maeve and Caitlin followed her–they were always left out, or so they claimed. But Hannah was happy to be with

Hamish once again, and the two of them ran up the mountain path, taking the route past the professor's croft and on to the plateau.

As they came over the brow, Hannah could see the hunting party on the far side of a ravine, which separated the paths. They paused, dropping down into the heathers so as not to be seen.

"Ye ran a long way from there to my mother's croft," Hannah said, and Hamish grinned at her.

"I told my uncle you'd help us flush out the stag," he said, and Hannah stared at him in disbelief.

"But… ye shouldnae have done that. I daenae want to see the creature hurt," she exclaimed, but Hamish shook his head.

"Neither do I. We can scare them back into the woods. My uncle won't realise. He's a terrible shot, and by the time he realises, they'll have gone. Look, can you see the herd from here?" he asked.

Hannah looked towards the treeline. It was hard to tell if the deer were there. She watched for a moment, and suddenly saw a hind, its white tail disappearing back into the woodland.

"They're there," she said, and Hamish squinted.

"I can't see them," he said, but now Hannah saw the entire herd coming towards the treeline.

There was the stag, with its magnificent antlers, and Hannah felt certain it was this creature whom Hamish's uncle would wish to see as his trophy. Across the ravine, a dog suddenly barked, and a volley of shots rang out towards the treeline.

To Hannah's relief, the herd darted back to safety amidst the trees, as several dogs now charged forward, yelping as they approached the woodland.

"They did nae hit anythin'–but they'll try again," Hannah said, watching as the duke called his men forward, sinking down into the heather as he did so.

"What can we do to stop them?" Hamish whispered.

"If we slip into the woodland, we could drive the herd back

down the hill. We could scare them ourselves," Hannah said, and Hamish nodded.

They retreated down the hill towards the professor's house, circling towards the woodland and entering it below the sight of the stalkers. It was a dangerous game to play–one false move and they, themselves, may be taken for a target.

It would be worth it if the stag was saved, and now they came in sight of the herd, grazing in a clearing a short distance away.

"We're downwind. They can't smell us," Hamish said, and Hannah nodded.

"That's right. They daenae know we're here. But we daenae want to drive them back towards the guns. We need to send them deeper into the woodland. This way," she said, and she led Hamish in an arc above where the deer were grazing until they were able to scare them in the right direction.

"I hated the idea of my uncle killing that magnificent creature. What right does he have to do it?" Hamish said, as now he and Hannah emerged from their hiding place into the clearing.

The deer looked up in surprise before darting away into the trees. But as they did so, a dozen shots rang out, and Hannah and Hamish were forced to lie flat on the ground and cover their heads. The scent of shot lingered in the air, but the herd was gone, and none of them had been hit.

"Tis' all right. They'll run for miles now," Hannah said, as the shouts of the stalkers could be heard behind them.

"They got away, my Lord," called out one of the men.

"Blast it, I thought I had the stag in my sights. We'll come back tomorrow," the duke called out, and the sounds of them retreating could now be heard.

Hannah and Hamish lay in the undergrowth for a short while, listening as the sounds of the hunting party grew distant. Hannah rose to her feet and sighed. They had saved the stag for one more day, but could they do so again? Hamish dusted himself off and grinned at Hannah.

"Wasn't that exciting? My uncle thinks he missed, but he had some help in doing so," he said, and Hannah nodded.

"I'm glad. I hate to see those wonderful creatures shot and dragged away for trophies," she said, shaking her head.

They began to climb back up through the woodland towards the moor. A light rain had set in, and Hannah suggested they return to the croft for bread and dripping, which had become Hamish's favourite. But as they came to the treeline, they heard a yelping sound–it was a hound, and it seemed to be in distress.

"It's one of the hunting dogs. It must have been caught in the shooting. Here, boy!" Hamish called out, and the hound let out another yelp.

It did not take long for them to find it. It was lying at the edge of the treeline, left behind when the rest of the hunting party retreated. Hannah kneeled at its side and stroked its head. It gave another yelp, and licked its paw, which was bleeding.

"A shot wound. We can carry it back to my mother's croft. We'll need to wash and bandage the paw. It'll be all right, though," Hannah said as Hamish lifted the dog into his arms.

It made no objection to this and allowed itself to be cradled as Hannah and Hamish made their way down the hill towards the croft. Hannah's mother was sitting outside with her darning, and she looked up in surprise as they approached.

"We found an injured hound, Mother. From the shootin' party," Hannah said, as her mother rose to her feet.

She tutted and shook her head.

"Tis' a terrible thing. These aristocrats. If tis' nae one thing they shoot, tis' another," she exclaimed, shaking her head.

Hannah blushed. Hamish was an aristocrat, and she felt embarrassed by the way in which her mother now spoke.

"Mother, please. Tis' Hamish ye speak of, too," she said, but her mother shook her head.

"Nay, tis' nae Hamish I speak of. Hamish is a boy. He doesnae share the bloodlust of his elders. Come now, we need to bathe the wound," she said, beckoning them to follow her inside.

Hannah's uncle was sitting by the fire, and he looked up in surprise as they entered, the dog giving a yelp, as though in greeting.

"What's this?" he asked.

"We found the dog in the woods, Uncle. He's injured–shot in the paw. He'll be all right. We need to clean and bandage the wound," Hannah said, as her two sisters looked on in fascination.

Her uncle nodded, and the dog was set down on the rug by the fire, as water was brought, along with a bandage to bind up the wound. Hannah and Hamish watched as Hanna's mother soothed the creature, gently stroking its head.

"There now, that's it, good as new," she said, and the dog barked as though in thanks.

"But what happens now, Mother?" Hannah asked, and her mother raised her eyebrows.

"Well… ye cannae send the poor creature back to its master. If a man can kill a stag, he can kill a lamed hound. It'll be of nay use anymore," she said, and Hannah glanced fearfully at Hamish, who nodded.

"That's right. He won't be welcome at the stables any longer. They're not pets. They're working dogs. He'd be… shot," he said, and Hannah gasped.

"We cannae let that happen, Mother," she said, and her mother shook her head.

"He can stay here. Once he's recovered, we'll see if Mr. McSween wants him. He'll be well trained, I'm sure. But make sure ye tell yer uncle, Hamish. I daenae want to be accused of stealin' a royal hound," Hannah's mother said, ruffling the dog's ears and rising to her feet.

The dog appeared quite content now, and allowed Hannah to carry it outside, where she and Hamish now sat in the late afternoon sunshine. Hannah smiled at the sight of the dog. Its head lolled to one side, and its tongue hanging out.

"Does it have a name?" she asked, but Hamish shook his head.

"None of the dogs have names. They're just gun dogs," he replied.

Hannah thought this was a terrible shame. Every dog deserved a name, and she thought hard about what they might name their new companion.

"What about… Sheppey?" she asked.

She did not know where she had plucked the name from, but it seemed to suit the docile creature lying happily in her arms, and Hamish nodded and smiled at her.

"Sheppey it is. I'll tell my uncle what's happened. I don't think he'll be particularly concerned. If the dog's happy," he said, and Hannah nodded.

"I'm glad we stopped them from killing the stag. I daenae know if we'll be so lucky next time," she said, and Hamish nodded.

"Yes, there's always another shooting party. If only the stags would learn to lie low. I know it's not as easy as that, though. And I'll not be here much longer to warn you when my uncle and the others are coming," he said, shaking his head sadly.

Hannah looked at him curiously. He had said nothing about going away. He had told her his home would be at Balmoral until the return of the Queen, and then he would either remain or go to his uncle's estate at Braemar, which was not far down the glen from where they sat.

"Are ye goin' somewhere?" she asked, and Hamish nodded sadly.

"I'm to be sent away to school. My uncle told me of the fact last night over dinner. I've been trying not to think about it," he said, sighing, and glancing at Hannah with a sorrowful look on his face.

Hannah was surprised by the feelings his words brought to

THE CROFTER'S DAUGHTER

her. She would miss him terribly. They had become close, and she had imagined them to be friends always.

"I... but where will he send ye? Will ye come back?" she asked, and Hamish shrugged.

"I'm to go to Gordonstoun. It's north of here–a school close to Elgin. My father went there. I'll come back during the holidays; I suppose. But… well, I'm not sure," he said, and Hannah nodded.

It seemed a cruel decision to make, even as Hamish had no choice in the matter.

"I'll miss ye," she said, and Hamish nodded.

"I'll miss you, too. I… well, I wasn't expecting to find a friend here. Not in such unexpected circumstances. But I'd better be going. I'll only get a scolding from Mimi if I'm later back," he said, ruffling Sheppey's ears.

The dog lolled on his back and raised his paws. Hamish rubbed his stomach, and Hannah was surprised to find tears welling up in her eyes. She did not want Hamish to leave. She knew they came from such different worlds, but they had found so much in common, and had shared so much already, their friendship blossoming like the spring flowers now growing across the moorland.

"I'll walk with ye. I can carry Sheppey back," Hannah said, and Hamish now lifted the dog into his arms, and the two of them walked along the moorland path in the direction of Balmoral.

As they came to the woodland, where the path forked down towards the castle, they met Connor coming the opposite way. He was surprised to see the dog in Hamish's arms, and when they had told him the story of what had happened, he smiled and shook his head.

"Yer uncle wasnae pleased to lose the shoot," he said, and Hannah and Hamish exchanged glances.

"But ye cannae agree with killin' the creatures, can ye, Connor?" Hannah asked, and her cousin shook his head.

"Nay, but tis' because of the stables I have a job. Men come from far and wide at the invitation of the estate. They expect to hunt. Besides, we need to control the deer numbers. They run amok in the forest, they eat the shoots of new trees – they're beautiful, but they're a nuisance, too – and there're plenty of them," he said.

"But they'd have shot the dog if it went back, wouldn't they?" Hannah said, and Connor nodded.

"Aye, I'm sure ye've done he creature a service by bandagin' it up and takin' care of it. I'd best be away," Connor said, and nodding to them, he hurried on up the path.

Hamish now handed Sheppey to Hannah, and once again she felt the tears welling up in her eyes, imagining this would be the last time she would see Hamish before he was sent away to school.

"Will ye… will ye come before ye go? To school, I mean?" she asked, and Hamish nodded.

"I will, yes. I'm supposed to leave at the end of the week. But I'll come before then, I promise. And I'll be back during the holidays. We can still have adventures, and you can teach Sheppey tricks whilst I'm away," he said, forcing a smile to his face, as Hannah nodded.

"I just thought… well, I thought you'd always be here," she replied, even as she knew such sentiments sounded foolish.

"And I'm only glad I met you, Hannah," he said, ruffling Sheppey's ears.

They bid one another goodbye, and Hannah watched him go, holding the dog in her arms, as tears rolled down her cheeks. She did not understand these new and unfamiliar feelings, and she was confused as to what they meant.

"I daenae want him to go, Sheppey," she said to the dog, who looked up at her with wide, loving eyes, and a tear rolled down her cheek.

THE TERRIBLE VICE

Hannah was trying her best not to think about Hamish's imminent departure. She had not shared her fears with her mother, but a few days later, as they were hanging washing on the line outside the house, Hannah began to cry.

She had not meant to cry. She had tried her best not to cry, but there was nothing she could do about it. Tears rolled down her cheeks, and she sank to the ground, as Sheppey came to sniff and paw at her.

"Hannah? What's the matter, lass? Why are ye cryin'–what's upset ye?" her mother asked, throwing the last of the clean washing over the line and coming to Hannah's side.

"Tis' nothin'–I'm all right," Hannah replied, but her mother tutted and shook her head.

"A lass doesnae cry for nothin'–what's wrong, Hannah? Has Hamish upset ye? I knew it was nae good for ye gettin' involved with such people. I bit my tongue, but…" she began, even as Hannah interrupted her.

"He's bein' sent away, Mother. He's goin' to some school in the north. I'm goin' to miss him so much," Hannah replied.

Her mother put her arms around her and kissed her on the forehead.

"There, there, Hannah. Tis' all right, I know why yer cryin'–tis' nothin' wrong with missin' someone ye've grown close to," she said, and Hannah nodded.

She did not understand why she was feeling like this. She had not cried like this when the professor had left, even as she had felt sad to see him go.

"But will he come back, Mother?" she asked, and her mother smiled.

"He might dae, Hannah. But ye mustn't worry if he doesn't. We all meet people we feel attached to. Tis' natural. Some stay, some go. This is the first time ye've felt like that about someone. Tis' a strange thing to feel like that, I know. But ye'll feel it again, I promise. And when Hamish goes, ye'll miss him, but ye'll get used to him nae bein' here, and… well, it'll get easier," her mother replied.

Hannah still felt confused. She did not know what feelings her mother was describing, only that it hurt terribly to think of Hamish going away.

"I've never missed someone like this before. Well, Father, but nae in the same way. Does that make me terribly selfish, Mother?" she asked, and her mother shook her head.

"Nay, Hannah. It makes ye the very opposite. Ye loved yer father, and I think yer in love with Hamish, too. But love comes in different forms–we love our parents in a way we daenae love our friends, tis' different. And we love those for whom we wish to spend our whole lives with differently still. Love is nae the same. Yer learnin' that today, Hannah," her mother said, and she kissed her on the top of her head and brought her more tightly into her embrace.

Hannah was still confused. She did not think she was in love with Hamish. She was only twelve years old, even as the feelings she had were of an intensity she had never known. If this was what being in love was like, then Hannah understood something of the anguish her mother had felt after Hannah's father's death.

Hamish was going away to school. He would be back, and surely, he would want to see her. But Hannah's mother had lost her husband–the man for whom she promised her whole life to.

"Mother, dae ye still miss Father?" Hannah asked, looking up at her mother, who nodded.

"Aye, I miss him every moment of the day. He's my last thought when I lay down to sleep, and my first when I awake. I love him… more than I can tell ye," she replied.

"But if that's what love does to ye, I daenae know if I want to fall in love. There's so much pain," Hannah said, and her mother smiled.

"Aye, but I'd go through it all again for the happiness we shared," she said, and she kissed Hannah again, holding her close, as the washing flapped in the breeze, and a tear rolled down Hannah's cheek.

* * *

IT WAS a day later when the familiar knock came at the door. Hamish had a particular way of knocking – three raps, a pause, and a final rap. Sheppey, too, had learned the knock, and with his paw healing well, he jumped up from his place by the fire and barked a shrill greeting.

"Oh, make him stop yappin'–I cannae sleep," Hannah's uncle called out from behind the curtain pulled across the bed.

"Tis' ten O'clock in the mornin'–ye should be up, Brendan," Hannah's aunt said, as Hannah hurried to open the door.

She had promised herself she would not cry, even as she knew Hamish was coming to say goodbye.

"Remember what I told ye, Hannah," her mother said, as Hannah opened the door.

But as she did so, she was surprised to find Hamish with tears in his own eyes, and he beckoned Hannah outside, as Sheppey barked and danced around his ankles.

"Enough, Sheppey. Come now, outside," Hannah said, and the dog followed her and Hamish onto the moorland path, where Hamish pointed up towards the professor's croft.

"Can we talk up there?" he said, and Hannah nodded.

They walked in silence up the mountain path. It was a bright spring day, and the wind was blowing the white clouds across the sky. From their vantage point, they could see right across the glen, the turrets of Balmoral rising below, and the curve of the river sparkling silver in the sunshine.

Sheppey ran ahead, and Hannah had to call him back, as the two of them came to the croft. The professor had still not returned, and they sat down under one of the trees as Hannah looked at Hamish curiously.

"Are ye goin' to tell me what's upset ye?" she asked, wondering if perhaps he, too, was sorry to be leaving her.

He turned to her and shook his head, sighing and putting his head in his hands and groaning. Sheppey sniffed at him, and Hannah put her arm around him, anxious to comfort him. She could not imagine what had so upset him.

"It's too terrible for words," he exclaimed.

"Has someone died? Have ye had some terrible news?" she asked, and he looked up at her and nodded.

"Not a death, but… a loss. It's my uncle. He's the kindest of men, and I begrudge nothing against him. But… he's a gambler. He always has been. It's a vice that's infected him these many years past. Late night card games, money on horses, all that sort of thing. He's lost and won over the years. But the stakes always grew higher. I wasn't so aware of it at first, but Mimi noticed the signs, too. He'd become withdrawn and forlorn after a loss or elated to the point of ecstasy. Anyway… last night, there was a gathering at Braemar, at my uncle's estate, my uncle, and several others. Unscrupulous men, and… well, my uncle lost at cards.

He'd put a wager on he couldn't ever afford. It's a gamble that's cost him… everything," Hamish said, sighing and lowering his head in shame.

Hannah could hardly believe what she was hearing. It was dreadful, and she shook her head, still with her arm around Hamish, who began to sob.

"But by everything, do you mean the estate?" she said, and Hamish nodded.

"That's right. He's lost the estate and all his fortune on one game of cards. He's lost everything. There's nothing left. I don't know how he could ever have been so foolish," Hamish exclaimed, and he stomped his foot in frustration, causing Sheppey to jump.

Hannah's thoughts turned to the school. If Hamish's uncle had lost his fortune, then did that mean Hamish, too, was penniless?

"But what of you? What happens to you? And Mimi? Are you still to be sent away to school?" she asked, but Hamish shook his head.

"No, I can't be sent away to school now. There's no money for the fees. My uncle can't afford to pay, and my own money, well… it seems he gambled that way, too. I'm penniless, just like him. I've got a title, but nothing to call my own. I live on charity– whatever that means. As for Mimi, she'll have to leave. I don't need a governess anymore, but… she's more than that. She's been like a mother to me. Oh, it's so awful," he exclaimed, gritting his teeth and clenching his fists.

Hannah sighed. She could only feel sorry for him, even as she felt glad he would not be leaving for Gordonstoun. But without his fortune, what future was there for the duke? And without the duke, what future was there for Hamish?

"But what happens now? Where's yer uncle?" she asked, anxious to know more about the terrible situation Hamish now found himself in.

"He's at Braemar. But the man he made the wager with is

taking the house. He's an unscrupulous man. He's threatened my uncle with ruin if he doesn't fulfil the terms of the bet. It was made in fairness. There were witnesses. My uncle wagered his entire fortune on a game of cards. I don't know what came over him. I don't know why he did it. I just know… well, we've lost everything. I've lost everything. I never wanted to go to that school, but my uncle was insistent. I wanted to stay here, with you, and now… I don't think I can do that, either. I don't know where I'll be sent. It's up to the Queen, isn't it?" Hamish said.

"It's up to ye, too. Ye cannae just be sent away," Hannah said, even as she feared the worst.

Sheppey put his paws up on Hamish's knees and barked. Hannah fondled the dogs' ears, and Hamish sighed, giving a weak smile as Sheppey licked his face.

"A dog doesn't care about wealth, does it? It doesn't care about title or position. It loves unconditionally. I do love my uncle, Hannah. But he's behaved in the most terrible way. It's a vice he can't rid himself of, and with every wager, he became more reckless, until…" Hamish said, his words trailing off as Hannah sighed.

"It'll be all right. They'll nae send ye away," she said, but Hamish shook his head.

"You don't know what they're like. My uncle brought scandal on the family. Prince Albert won't like it. He'll see my uncle sent somewhere quietly out of the way, or worse… they'll put us both in the poorhouse. What other choice do we have? We've got nothing, Hannah. I'm as poor as you… I'm sorry, I didn't mean to say that," he said, blushing and turning away, but Hannah smiled.

He was right. She was poor and having never known what it was like to be rich, Hannah had no means of telling what it would be like to lose a fortune. She could imagine gaining one–the gift of the gold sovereign which Hamish's uncle had so kindly given her felt like that. But to lose a fortune, that was something else.

"We're poor. We have nothin' but the clothes we stand up in, and a few odds and ends. But that doesnae mean ye cannae be happy, Hamish. It means a different life, but nae a bad one. They'll nae send ye away. Tis' yer uncle who did this. Nae ye," Hannah said, even as she was uncertain of her own words.

In truth, she could not say what the Royal Family would do, and as she and Hamish sat in front of the professor's croft that afternoon, it seemed the future was bleak.

"I just wish… well, maybe it's easier to be born with nothing. That way, you can't lose it," Hamish said, rising to his feet, as Sheppey jumped at him and barked.

"Yer uncle will nae abandon ye, Hamish. He'll have to help ye," Hannah said, but Hamish only shrugged.

"I don't know, Hannah. I don't know where I'll go, or what they'll make me do," he said, turning to her.

She reached out and took his hand in hers. She squeezed it, smiling weakly at him and sighing.

"Ye can stay here, with us, if ye need to," she said, and he returned her smile and shook his head.

"You're very kind, Hannah. I don't know what I've done to deserve a friend like you. We aristocrats don't always make the best friends–at least… I've not found many people who really wanted to be my friend. They were more interested in my money, and now I don't have that, either. It seems I'll never have any friends," he replied.

But Hannah had never seen it like that. She had seen the differences between them, but also the many things they shared. They were just two children, brought together by circumstance. She wanted to be his friend, not for any gain on her part, but because he, too, was a friend to her.

"But we're friends, aren't we?" she said, and he nodded.

"I don't know why you'd want to be my friend, Hannah," he replied, but Hannah squeezed his hand, and leaning up, she kissed him on the cheek.

"Because I dae," she replied.

He was about to reply when there came a call from the path below. Hannah turned, and she was delighted to see the professor, puffing, and panting up the mountain path, leading a pony, which also appeared to be struggling under the weight of several large saddle bags.

"Goodness me, what a hike. A winter of sittin' at a desk at the university does nothin' for a man's constitution. How wonderful to see ye, Hannah," he exclaimed, and Hannah ran to greet him.

"Professor Lochray. Oh, I've missed ye so much," she exclaimed, throwing her arms around the professor and kissing him on both cheeks.

"And I've missed ye, too," the professor replied.

He pulled out a handkerchief and mopped his brow, as Sheppey came to dance around his ankles.

"This is Sheppey, Professor, and this is Hamish… Lord Beaufort," Hannah said, embarrassed at having introduced Hamish in such informal terms.

Hamish stepped forward, and the professor held out his hands

"Tis' a pleasure to meet ye, sir. I've read of ye. I'm sorry for the loss of yer parents," he said, and Hamish nodded.

"It was some years ago now. But thank you. I hope you don't mind us sitting outside your croft," Hamish said, glancing at Hannah as he spoke, but the professor shook his head.

"Nay, of course nae. When I'm nae here, tis' Hannah's croft– the garden at least. But how good it feels to be back in the fresh air of the highlands," he said, taking a deep breath.

Hannah took out the box containing the butterfly the professor had given her. He smiled at her and nodded.

"I always keep it with me, Professor," she said, opening the box to reveal the butterfly, perfectly preserved inside.

"And I've new ones to show ye, too. But why the glum faces on ye both? Ye look like lost souls," the professor said.

Hannah closed the case and glanced at Hamish, who shook his head sadly.

"I've had some bad news, Professor. It's my uncle–the Duke of Braemar. He's lost a fortune at the card table. His whole fortune. He's left with nothing. I'm left with nothing. I'm fearful for the future," Hamish said, and the professor pondered for a moment.

He beckoned for them both to sit down outside the croft, and unburdening the pony of its saddle bags, he sat down next to them and sighed.

"Tis' a vicious vice–that of the gambler. I had it myself," he said, fondling Sheppey's ears.

Hannah looked at him in amazement. The professor had never mentioned such a vice to her, even as she realised how little she knew of his past. She knew him as the kindly eccentric who inhabited the hillside each summer. But as for his life in Edinburgh, she knew nothing.

"Ye were a gambler, too, Professor?" she asked, and the professor nodded.

"Aye, Hannah. And I lost everythin' through it. Tis' a terrible narcotic. First a small wager here and there, then another, then another. Before ye know it, ye've lost everythin' ye have, and there's nothin' left for ye," he said.

Hamish shook his head–it was precisely what had happened to his uncle, and Hannah reached out and slipped her hand into his.

"But ye've nae lost everythin' now, have ye?" she said.

"Nay, Hannah. And that's why I'm tellin' ye this story. A man can lose everythin' and gain it again. Yer uncle will, too, Hamish. It will nae be like this forever. I thought I'd never get my money back. But bit by bit, I have conquered my troubles. Sometimes, we need to lose everythin' to realise the things we have," the professor replied.

Hannah was grateful to him for his honesty, and he put his hand gently on her shoulder and smiled.

"But I don't know what to do now," Hamish said, and the professor shook his head.

"It's nae for ye to decide, sir. Yer still young. Daenae take the cares of the world on yer shoulders just yet. They'll nae see ye stray far," the professor said, and now he rose to his feet, and Sheppey barked and jumped up at him.

Hannah and Hamish, too, rose to their feet, and Hannah felt eager to ease Hamish's anxieties. She felt terribly sorry for him and wanted to do something to comfort and reassure him.

"Think about the butterflies, Hamish. Daenae they start as nothin' more than caterpillars and then become somethin' beautiful?" she said.

The professor laughed and nodded.

"Hannah's right. And that's why I found such beauty in the butterflies myself. I had nothin' and bit by bit, with a great deal of effort, I gained what I have now. I'm happy. I daenae have a fortune, but I'm content. I spend my summers here amidst the beauty of the highlands. A man cannae buy such beauty. Money only goes so far. Ye'll be all right, Hamish, and yer blessed with a good friend, in Hannah. She's been a good friend to me, and she'll be a good friend to ye, too," he said.

Sheppey jumped up at Hamish, and he ruffled his ears, giving a weak smile, as Hannah beckoned him to follow her.

"We'd better be goin'–they'll wonder where we are," she said, and Hamish nodded.

"Thank you, Professor," he said, and the professor smiled.

"Come and visit me anytime ye wish. I'll be here–or out on the moorland. I've a whole summer ahead of me. Just me and the butterflies. That's how I like it," he said, and with a cheery wave, he bid them goodbye.

Hannah and Hamish walked slowly down the path back towards Hannah's mother's croft. Hamish was still subdued, and Hannah could only imagine the fear and trepidation in his heart.

She did not know what it was like to lose a fortune. She had never possessed one, nor did she believe she ever would. But she *could* understand the fear of loss–she feared losing her mother, or one of her sisters, her aunt or uncle. She had lost her father, and she knew well enough what such a loss felt like.

"It'll be all right, Hamish," she repeated, even as she knew her words surely sounded hollow and empty to one who believed they had lost everything, but Hamish paused, turning to her with a smile on his face.

"The professor's words made me feel a great deal better. He's right–we can lose everything, but some things remain. I've not lost you, have I? I've not lost my senses, or my wonder at the world. I've not lost those things which make me who I am," he said, and Hannah smiled.

"That's right–and ye cannae lose those things, Hamish. They're a part of ye, and nay one can take them away from ye," she replied.

"I suppose I should go back to the castle. They'll be wondering where I am. I felt so sorry for Mimi. She looked so upset this morning," Hamish said, as they came in sight of the croft.

"Will ye still come and see me?" Hannah asked, slipping her hand into his.

He smiled at her and nodded.

"How could I not? I never wanted to go to that stupid school. I wanted to stay here with you. I'm glad about that, at least," he said, and Hannah smiled back at him.

"And I'm glad, too," she replied.

She watched him go, standing by the door of the croft. Her mother came out to hang some washing on the line, and she looked at Hannah inquisitively.

"What was Hamish upset about?" she asked, and Hannah put her arms around her mother and rested her head on her shoulder.

"He's lost everythin'–his uncle's gambled it all away," she said, and her mother sighed.

"Tis' a terrible curse–the gambler's curse," she said, and Hannah nodded.

But she could not help but feel somewhat relieved at the thought of Hamish remaining close by – as selfish as it seemed. She would have missed him terribly if he had gone, and now that he was to remain at Balmoral, she wondered what the future held for them both.

THE GILLIE

News of Hamish's uncle's misfortune soon spread across the glen. The estate at Braemar was to be broken up and sold to pay the debts.

The man who had won the wager against the duke was demanding money–he did not want to be saddled with the estate, and the house and lands were up for sale.

Hamish still resided at Balmoral, but the scandal had engulfed him, too, and he would not be allowed to remain there for long. He was like a ship without a sail, directionless, and without purpose. He was now fourteen years old and had only his title and the clothes he stood up in.

Mimi had been sent away, and Hannah now stood watching the sad moment of her departure, as Hamish had clung to her, vowing to bring her back when his fortune was restored.

"But you won't need a governess then, Master Hamish," she said to him, but Hamish shook his head and kissed her on the cheeks.

"No, but I'll still need my friends, Mimi," he told her, as now she climbed into the carriage and looked forlornly from the window as it drew away from the front of the house.

As Hamish stood watching, Hannah went up and slipped her hand into his, squeezing it and trying to reassure him.

"It'll be all right," she whispered, but he turned to her and shook his head.

"I feel as though everything I've known is being dismantled bit by bit. I watched the castle being built, and now I feel I'm being taken apart. My uncle's estate is soon to be sold. There's no money for anything. I'm like a bird in a gilded cage. There's talk of me being sent away. But they don't know what to do with me. And now Mimi's gone, too. It's as though there's nothing familiar left," he said, shaking his head.

"But ye've still got me, and the professor, and Mr. McSween, and my mother, and the rest of my family," Hannah said.

Hamish smiled and nodded.

"And I'm grateful for that. But I know what your mother thinks of me. She only tolerates me because of you," Hamish replied.

Hannah blushed. She had not realised Hamish was aware of her mother's feelings towards the Royal Family, even as she knew her mother would never have voiced them in Hamish's presence.

"'Tis' nae true, Hamish. My mother… she blames the Royal Family for what happened to my father. But she doesnae blame ye for it," she said, but Hamish shook his head.

"I'm not wanted anywhere… I'm sorry, Hannah. I'm not very good company now. I'll come and see you tomorrow," he said, and he wandered off across the castle forecourt, leaving Hannah standing alone.

She sighed and shook her head, watching his forlorn figure make its way inside. She wanted to help him, but there was nothing she could do. With a heavy heart, Hannah returned home.

She was watching another person lose everything, just as she had felt as though she, too, had lost everything following the death of her father. It was painful, and she could only feel sorry for everything Hamish was going through.

As she came in sight of the croft, her two younger sisters came running towards her. They looked anxious, grabbing her hand, and pulling her towards home.

"What's the matter? What's happened?" she asked.

"Tis' Uncle, he's fallen. Mother thinks he's broken his leg," Maeve exclaimed, and Hannah followed them towards the croft, just as Connor emerged with an anxious expression on his face.

"I'm goin' to fetch the doctor. My father's in a bad way," he said, and he ran off in the direction of the castle.

Inside, all was chaos and confusion. Hannah's uncle was lying on the bed, screaming in pain, as her mother and aunt rushed back and forth, trying their best to help.

"What happened, Mother?" Hannah asked, hurrying to her mother's side.

"Yer uncle fell. That's what happened. He shouldnae have been tryin' to get up without help. He's a stubborn man," she exclaimed, shaking her head, and glaring at Hannah's uncle, who was biting on a piece of wood as Hannah's aunt tried to dress the wound.

"Hold still, Brendan," she exclaimed.

"I'm holdin' still, woman. I cannae help the pain, can I?" he cried out, as Hannah went to his side.

"Connor's gone to fetch the doctor, Uncle," she said, and her uncle let out an angry cry.

"What use is that? I daenae need a doctor. What's he goin' to dae? Charge for the privilege of his opinion?" he exclaimed, spitting out the piece of wood as he spoke.

"Yer somethin' else, Brendan, ye really are," Hannah's aunt exclaimed.

This scene continued for the rest of the afternoon until eventually Connor arrived with the doctor. He demanded a handsome fee for the consultation, which, as Hannah's uncle had predicted, was merely a matter of assessment, rather than action.

"Aye, it's broken," he said, rising to his feet and addressing Hannah's aunt.

"I know it's broken. What can ye dae about it?" Hannah's uncle demanded.

The doctor raised his eyebrows.

"Ye'll need an operation, Mr. McGinn. Nae a pleasant one, either. The bone needs settin' right. If tis' left to heal, ye'll have a crooked leg," he replied.

"And can ye dae that operation, Doctor?" Hannah's aunt asked.

The doctor shook his head.

"Nay. Tis' an operation to be done by surgeons, nae in a remote highland croft. Ye summoned me here. That's my opinion," he said, taking up his medical bag.

"And ye expect us to pay ye for yer opinion, dae ye?" Hannah's uncle exclaimed.

"Brendan," her aunt hissed.

The doctor sighed and shook his head.

"I'm nae a surgeon, Mr. McGinn. I'm a physician. I'm tellin' ye what ye need, but I'm afraid it cannae be done here. Tis' a costly business, medicine. It requires skill and trainin'–it cannae be performed by amateurs. Now, ye could have the operation in Edinburgh. The bone needs to be set. If it heals now, ye'll walk with a limp for the rest of yer life. My suggestion is ye wait until ye've enough money, then have the operation performed later," he said.

Hannah's uncle fell silent. Hannah knew they could never afford an operation like that. Such things were for those with money–not the likes of them.

"Thank ye, Doctor. We'll think about it," Hannah's aunt said, as she saw the doctor to the door.

"If ye need any further advice, I'm happy to be consulted," the doctor replied.

"Aye, for another fee," Hannah's uncle called after him.

The door closed, and Hannah's aunt rounded on him, pointing her finger at him angrily. Her aunt rarely raised her voice, and Hannah was surprised to see the anger in her eyes.

"That's enough, Brendan. He was tryin' to help ye, but yer too stubborn to see that. Ye need an operation. We cannae afford it. Tis' a matter of fact. What did ye expect him to dae? Fix yer leg by magic?" she exclaimed, turning away with tears in her eyes.

Hannah's mother went to put her arms around her, and she began to sob. Hannah ushered Maeve and Caitlin outside, where they sat on the low bench by the door, and Sheppey jumped up at them and barked.

"Why is Aunt Rose so sad?" Maeve asked.

"Because she wants Uncle Brendan to get better. But he will nae get better without an operation on his leg. Tis' nay one's fault, but tis' a tragedy all the same," Hannah replied.

She was fondling Sheppey's ears, but as she looked up, she saw a figure coming towards the croft along the moorland path. It was Hamish, and she smiled at him as he approached. He, too, looked downcast, and it seemed a cloud was about to rest over the house for the rest of the day.

"I've got news," he said, as Hannah went to meet him, leaving her sisters playing with Sheppey.

"Is everythin' all right? Is it yer uncle?" Hannah asked.

"Shall we walk across the moors?" he asked.

Hannah called for Sheppey, though she forbade her sisters from coming with them. They sat grumpily on the bench as Hannah and Hamish walked along the bridleway in the direction of Mr. McSween's farm.

"What's happened?" she asked, and Hamish turned to her and sighed.

"I'm to leave Balmoral. Prince Albert wrote to my uncle. He's angry about the scandal–it's brought shame to the Royal Family. My uncle was trusted with overseeing the estate in the absence of the Queen, but he's betrayed that trust. I'm not allowed to remain there any longer. I'm to go to Braemar, but… the house is for sale. My uncle… he stays in the library all day, drinking brandy. He's terribly depressed. I've never seen him like this before," Hamish said.

"My uncle's the same–he's broken his leg. The doctor came, but he needs an operation. He's a terrible patient, and he's shoutin' at my aunt, and she's shoutin' back at him. But what happens now? If the estate at Braemar is goin' to be sold, where will ye go?" Hannah asked.

She was glad to be walking with Hamish across the moorland, even as they had both brought their troubles with them.

"I don't know. I'll have to get a job–labouring on a farm, maybe. I wonder if Mr. McSween might take me," he said.

Hannah could not believe what she was hearing–the nephew of a duke, reduced to begging jobs on a farm.

"But ye cannae dae that," she said.

Hamish looked somewhat affronted, as though she was suggesting he was incapable of such work.

"But I can labour. I'm not afraid of hard work," he replied, but Hannah shook her head.

"I daenae mean that. But yer to be a duke, there must be some other way," she said.

Hamish pondered for a moment, appearing somewhat embarrassed, even as Hannah looked at him curiously.

"There is one other thought I had, but I'll need your help," he said, and she smiled at him.

"I'll help ye anyway I can," she replied.

"I thought I could be a gillie," he said.

* * *

HAMISH'S PLAN TO act as a gillie on the estate was not as farfetched as it might have seemed. He knew a great deal about the wildlife on the estate, and the next morning, he came to the croft early, so that Hannah might teach him more about stalking.

"I daenae like the work "stalk"–I daenae want to see the creatures killed. But I'll teach ye to follow them. Tis' easy enough," she said, as they set out with Sheppey across the moors.

It was another bright spring day. The clouds were high in the sky, and there was a fair breeze blowing across the heathers. Instead of climbing up past the professor's croft, they took a route which led them towards Mr. McSween's farm.

They passed the site of the accident with the pony, before climbing up onto a large swathe of moorland which looked south towards high mountains in the far distance. Hannah had never been further than the edge moor on this side of the croft.

What lay beyond was a mystery, and the two of them now walked for about a mile, to a place where Hannah had often watched the stags.

"Do you think I'd make a good gillie? I know I don't know as much as you do, but I'm willing to learn," he said, and Hannah laughed.

"I've never wanted to a be a gillie. I daenae think lasses can be gillies. But I know the wildlife on the moorlands well enough. Look above ye–can ye see the eagle circlin' up there?" she said, pointing up to where an eagle was soaring high above them.

Hamish looked up in amazement and nodded.

"I see it. But I wasn't looking. How did you spot it?" he asked, and Hannah smiled.

Her father had taught her to always be observant–looking up, and side to side, always on the watch.

"Ye've got to keep yer eyes open. Look in every direction," she said, as now the eagle swooped down towards the glen.

"I don't pay attention. That's my problem. I don't see the details," Hamish replied, looking suddenly forlorn.

"But ye can teach yerself the details. Keep lookin'–observe everythin' ye see," she said, and Hamish nodded.

"I'll try. Are there any stags nearby?" he asked.

Hannah paused, gazing out across the wide expanse of heathers. A ravine, where a stream gushed from a high waterfall, obscured a place where the deer often congregated, and she beckoned Hamish to follow her, approaching downwind, and reminding him of the need to always keep out of the scent of whatever quarry was being pursued.

"Animals have a far greater sense of smell than we dae. They can smell us from miles away. But we can use the wind to our advantage. Stay downwind of the animal. That way, our scent is carried away on the very breeze the animal relies on for scent," Hannah said, as they approached the edge of the ravine.

"So, we always need to be aware of the wind direction?" Hamish said, and Hannah nodded.

"That's right, always stay downwind. But look, there they are," she said, crouching low, and pointing through the heathers to where a herd was grazing at the edge of the stream.

There were perhaps two dozen deer, all standing together, whilst a large stag stood proudly high on a rock, looking down on the herd below. If they had been stalkers, the herd would not have stood a chance.

"I can't believe who close we are," Hamish exclaimed, and Hannah beckoned him to creep forward a little.

"We can get quite close," she said as they used the heather to conceal themselves, moving forward little by little.

A line of rocks separated them from the edge of the stream, and none of the herd had noticed them, as now they crept forward still further. Hannah's heart was beating fast–she loved the thrill of getting close to any creature, but particularly the deer.

She could see the stag in all his magnificence, the monarch of the glen, looking out over his kingdom.

"Look at them," Hamish exclaimed.

But the sound of his voice echoed in the ravine, causing the herd to look up. Fear and panic now ensued, and the creatures scattered in every direction, charging back out onto the heathers, as Hannah and Hamish cowered beneath the rock behind which they had been hiding. As the stag darted away, Hannah rose breathlessly to her feet and dusted herself down.

"That's what happens when ye talk," she said, and Hamish sighed.

"I'm sorry. I didn't mean to startle them away like that," he exclaimed, and Hannah smiled at him.

"If ye want to be a gillie, ye need to learn how to get close and stay quiet. Tis' the only way," she said, and Hamish nodded.

He sat down on a rock by the stream and tossed a pebble idly into the water, where it splashed.

"I don't think I'll be very good at it. I'm sorry, Hannah. I shouldn't have raised my voice–I scared them away," he said, but Hannah shook her head and smiled.

"It's all right. Yer still learnin'–my father used to take me out to watch the deer. He could follow them for miles. He would get so close to them, then slip away without them ever knowin' he was there, and... oh, where's Sheppey?" she asked.

The dog had been following them earlier that morning, but in the excitement of following the herd, Hannah had forgotten all about him. They looked around them for any sign of him, calling to him, but to no avail.

"Sheppey? Come here, boy. Where are you?" Hamish called out, as they climbed out of the ravine and onto the moorland.

But there was no sign of Sheppey anywhere, and as they approached Hannah's mother's croft, they feared he was lost on the moor.

"When did ye last see him?" Hannah asked, and Hamish scratched his head.

"Well, when we set out. But I don't remember seeing him

when we watched the eagle. I should've been watching out for him. But I was too busy looking for the deer," Hamish replied.

Hannah felt anxious. She loved Sheppey, and the thought of him lost on the moor was terrible.

"Sheppey?" she called out, vaguely hoping he might hear her.

But as she did so, a yelp came from the path above, and looking up, she saw the dog running towards her, followed by Professor Lochray, who waved to them as he approached.

"I think I've found somethin' belongin' to the two of ye," he said, as Sheppey came bounding up, yelping, and jumping at Hamish, who grinned at him.

"Good dog, Sheppey. We've been terribly worried about you," he said, and the professor laughed.

"He was stalkin' me. I kept thinkin' I saw a movement in the heathers. I've been out all night lookin' for moths, and I lost track of time. Moth huntin' turned to butterfly huntin'–and then it seemed I was bein' hunted myself," he said, smiling at Sheppey, who was now lying on his back and waggling his legs in the air.

"Good dog, Sheppey. We've been looking for you for the past hour. We thought you'd followed us," Hamish said, and the dog looked up at him, as if to say his disappearance was obvious.

He had gone to his friend, the professor, who now stooped down to ruffle the dog's ears.

"I'll be sure to return him if he finds his way to my side again," the professor said, and Hannah and Hamish thanked him for his kindness.

"Hannah's been trying to teach me how to be a gillie," Hamish said, and the professor raised his eyebrows.

"Are you bein' sent away from Balmoral, sir?" he asked, and Hamish nodded.

"There's no money, and my uncle's caused a scandal. The Royal Family doesn't like scandals. I thought about getting a job on one of the farms, but then I thought I might become a gillie instead," Hamish replied.

It was a sad end to noble prospects, and Hannah could only feel terribly sorry for Hamish, reduced in circumstances to the possibility of being nothing but a glorified servant.

"Well, I wish ye luck, Hamish. I'm sorry about what's happened, and I only hope yer uncle can recover from what's happened – nae only his fortune, but his dignity, too," the professor replied.

He went of whistling to himself, his butterfly net slung over his shoulder, and Hannah and Hamish sat down outside the croft with Sheppey. The door opened, and Hannah's mother appeared, carrying a plate with bread and dripping on it.

"A long walk deserves a good feed," she said, smiling at them as she placed the plate on the bench between them.

"That's very kind of you, Mrs. McGinn," Hamish said, and Hannah's mother smiled.

"I know yer nae havin' an easy time now, Hamish. I have nae always given ye the friendliest of welcomes, but I'm grateful to ye for yer friendship towards Hannah. Take good care of yerself. Yer always welcome here," she said, before returning inside.

Hamish smiled at Hannah, who slipped her hand into his and squeezed it.

"Ye see, tis' nae the end," she replied, taking a piece of bread and dripping and returning his smile.

TRAGEDY STRIKES

Hannah's uncle's condition did not improve. He would lie in bed, lamenting his lot, his leg healing only partially, so it became obvious the operation was necessary, even as they could not afford it.

Even if they saved everything they had, the cost was beyond their reach, and Hannah's uncle became ever more bitter with each passing day. He blamed everyone–the Royal Family included–and there was not a day went by when he and Hannah's aunt did not exchange a cross word or insult.

Hannah grew tired of their constant bickering, and a cloud of sorrow seemed to hang over the croft. But Hannah had her own concerns, and she was determined to do all she could to help Hamish in his troubles.

It was a month since the Duke of Braemar had lost everything at the gambling table. Hamish had been told to leave Balmoral, though he had been offered a job alongside Connor in the stables–a humiliation for one such as him, but, it seemed, his only choice.

He had taken the job, and was working hard, even as he had told Hannah how alien it felt to be a servant in the house he had once been master. Hannah visited him regularly at the stables—if only to get away from the constant arguments at the croft, and on this morning, she was walking with her cousin in the direction of the castle, sharing the sadness they both were living through.

"I feel so sorry for my father, but he shouldnae shout at my mother like that. She cannae mend his leg. Tis' only an operation can dae that, and we cannae afford the operation," Connor said, kicking at a tuft of grass along the bridleway.

It was a beautiful day—the first flush of summer was in the air, and the sun was warm on Hannah's face as they walked.

"But he will nae listen, will he? He will nae be told. Men are stubborn," Hannah replied.

Connor turned to her and smiled.

"Dae ye mean me as well?" he asked, and Hannah laughed.

She and her cousin were close. She loved him deeply, and the two of them had endured much together.

"Perhaps nae ye. But most men," she said, and Connor smiled.

"Aye, yer right. And my father is the worst. But we cannae afford the operation. He's nae goin' to have it," Connor said, shaking his head.

Hannah's uncle had not allowed the doctor to return. He had stubbornly refused him, and it seemed to Hannah as though he was happier complaining than trying to help himself.

Her mind was elsewhere, and as they approached the castle, she was looking forward to seeing Hamish, even if his circumstances were drastically reduced.

"Is Hamish still workin' hard?" she asked, as they approached the stables, which lay behind the main house in an ornately designed block.

Connor nodded.

"He works hard, aye. But tis' strange to see him there. The other grooms, too... they daenae know what to say to him. He rides back to Braemar on the nights he does nae sleep here. I fear for him, though," Connor said.

Hannah looked curiously at her cousin. She did not understand what he meant, even as she was fearful for Hamish, too. He had lost everything, and with his uncle descending into a spiral of depression and self-loathing, she felt uncertain as to the future.

"How so?" she asked, as they made their way under the stable arch and into the stable yard.

"I hope he doesnae go the same way as his uncle. The grooms play cards, and… well, tis' always a temptation," Connor replied.

Hannah looked around her. The stables were always busy – the royal stud being exercised, or well-dressed gentlemen coming to ride out.

The previous day there had been a hunt, and Hannah had watched as Hamish saw off the horses which would carry the men up onto the moors, from which they would then set off on foot in search of their quarry.

Hamish himself now appeared from one of the stables, and he smiled at her as she hurried over to him.

"Are ye all right?" she asked, and he nodded.

"I'm all right. I've just been mucking out one of the horse's stalls. He's a fine creature. But I must confess to feeling a little miserable this morning," he said, sighing, as Hannah put her hand on his arm.

"Tis' nay surprise ye feel miserable. None of this is yer fault, Hamish. Ye must feel so humiliated workin' here, after…" she began, but before she could finish, the equerry who had brought news of Hannah's father's death, and that of her uncle's pension, appeared in the stable yard.

He looked around him, his eyes resting on Hamish, to whom he now beckoned.

"What does he want?" Hamish whispered.

"I daenae know. But he wants to speak to ye," Hannah replied.

She watched as Hamish went over to the equerry, unable to hear what was being said. But there was no doubt it was something bad–Hamish let out a sudden cry of anguish, and the equerry caught him by the shoulders, speaking harshly to him, even as Hamish tried to pull away.

Hannah hurried over, and now she heard the equerry's harsh tones as he pointed to Hamish with a scowl on his face.

"He's dead, Hamish. That's it. The house, the estate, it'll all be sold," he said, and Hamish turned away with tears rolling down his cheeks.

"What's happened?" Hannah exclaimed, as the equerry walked away, shaking his head.

Hamish put his arms around Hannah, sobbing onto her shoulder as she clutched at him, not knowing how to comfort him.

"He's dead, Hannah. My uncle. He's dead. I wasn't there… I knew he was suffering; I knew he was growing weak. It was the worry that caused it. He didn't know what to do – but it's killed him," he sobbed, clinging to Hannah, who held him to her as tears rolled down her own cheeks, too.

"It's all right, Hamish. It's all right," she said, even as she knew it was not all right, and never would be.

With Hamish's uncle dead, he was all alone. His parents had died in India, Mimi had been sent back to London, and the Royal Family had cast him aside–as much a part of the scandal as his uncle. He had nothing, reduced from riches to rags.

"It's not all right, Hannah. I've got nothing left. What can I do?" he said, as he stepped back and gazed into Hannah's eyes with an imploring look on his face.

"We'll find a way," Hannah replied, even as she did not know what that way would be.

* * *

IT WAS LATER that afternoon when a horse and trap arrived from Braemar, bearing the few possessions left by Hamish's uncle. Everything else was to be sold, and there remained only a box containing a set of paintings–six in total, some candlesticks, a few shirts, and pairs of breeches, along with a box of books. This was all that was left of the Braemar estate, even as the title itself passed to Hamish.

"Yer the Duke of Braemar?" Hannah asked, after the equerry had left them with the news and contents of the boxes.

"That's right. I was my uncle's ward. He had no children or closer relatives. But what's the point of a title when you've nothing to show for it? Oh... I wish he'd told me how he was feeling. I wish he'd told me the truth," Hamish said, shaking his head sadly.

"Perhaps he did nae want to worry ye," Hannah replied.

Hamish laughed and sighed.

"Well, he has now, hasn't he? Look at this stuff. A few worthless paintings, a couple of candlesticks, and some moth-eaten clothes. And these books... *The Pelagian Heresy, The Annals of Horatio, The Articles of the Council of Trent, The Empire of Byzantine*... what do I want with these?" Hamish exclaimed, tossing the books he had picked out of the box idly to the ground.

Hannah picked them up and returned them to the others. The paintings were not without their merit–six small portrait studies, which might have looked nice, hung in a dressing room, or on a flight of stairs.

But Hamish had neither a dressing room nor a flight of stairs. He had nothing–except the contents of the cart and the clothes he stood up in.

"But what happens now? They'll sell the house to clear the gambling debt?" Hannah asked, and Hamish nodded.

"That's right. There won't be anything left over after that. Not at all," he said, sighing and leaning against the cart.

He was only fourteen years old, and now it seemed he bore

the weight of the world on his shoulders.

"And where will ye live?" she asked.

"I suppose I'll have to sleep in the hayloft here. There's nothing much more I can do, is there?" he replied.

"You could come to live with us," Hannah replied.

The idea had been at the back of her mind for some time, even as she had not discussed it with her mother or the rest of her family. Hamish looked at her in surprise.

"With you?" he said, and Hannah nodded.

"Ye cannae live in the hayloft for the rest of your life. Ye could live with us and contribute to the family. I know tis' nae what yer used to, but it would be better than livin' in the hayloft of the house ye once were master of–in the Queen's absence, I mean," Hannah replied.

Hamish thought for a moment. But what choice did he have? Hannah was glad to think she could help him, even as she knew it was far from ideal. She knew her mother would say yes, and that the rest of the family–even her uncle–would welcome Hamish, too.

"It's very kind of you, but can I really? I don't want to impose on you. It seems… wrong," he said, but Hannah shook her head.

"Tis' nay imposition. We're friends. Are we nae? Ye can live with us and work here on the estate. We can walk Sheppey every day, and, well… I'd like it if ye did," she said, and Hamish smiled.

"I'd like it, too. Oh… my poor uncle. I just can't believe… I don't want to believe he's dead," he said, and a tear rolled down his cheek.

Hannah slipped her hand into his and squeezed it. She hated to see him sad, even as he had every reason to cry after all that had happened to him.

"Ye daenae have to be alone, Hamish. Ye can live with us. Ye can be part of our family," she said, and he nodded.

"I'd like that. If you're sure your mother won't mind," he said.

"Then let's go and ask her," Hannah replied.

***

HANNAH AND HAMISH carried the boxes from the cart between them. They were awkward, and Hamish was all in favour of throwing their contents away.

"I don't need the books, Hannah," he said, setting down the box containing the volumes inherited from his uncle and sighing.

"But ye might dae–one day. Tis' a shame to throw away the last few things which remind ye of him," Hannah replied.

Hamish shook his head, pulling out one of the books and flicking through it.

"I don't want to be reminded of all this. I just feel… oh, I don't know what I feel. I'm so sad that he's gone, but I'm angry with him, too. Does that even make sense?" he asked, as Hannah put down the box she was carrying and turned to him.

"It does make sense, aye. Ye loved yer uncle, but he's left ye destitute. He's left ye with nothin' and now… well, ye have to start again. But daenae discard it all, Hamish. Tis' worth keepin' yer memories. I have nothin' to remind me of my father. I wish did, and sometimes I feel angry at him for leavin' us behind. I love him, but… I wish he had nae done what he did," Hannah replied.

She had never voiced those feelings before, but it was how she felt. Her father had made a mistake in poaching from the royal estate, and it had cost him his life.

He had left behind a family who had struggled terribly in the years since his death. Hannah would never have said as much to her mother, but her father was responsible for much of their suffering, even as Hannah missed him terribly.

"You're right–it's possible to love someone, even when you don't like the things they've done," Hamish replied.

"So daenae get rid of the boxes, Hamish. Ye'd regret it later," Hannah said, taking out one of the paintings from the box she had been carrying and holding it up to look at.

It was a study of a woman–a young woman, with a pale face and large, blue eyes. She was very pretty, her neck surrounded by a starched ruff and high collar, her hair short and drawn back. Her lips were bright red, and she was looking only slightly towards the painter, the background dark.

All six of the paintings were of the same woman, and Hannah was curious as to who she might be.

"I think they're horrible," Hamish said, peering over Hannah's shoulder.

"Dae ye? I think they're rather good. She's very pretty, though stern lookin' in her face," Hannah said, and Hamish laughed.

"You're welcome to them if you want them. I doubt anyone saw any value in them. They'd have taken them otherwise. My uncle's house at Braemar was filled with treasures–he's lost a staggering amount of money," Hamish said, shaking his head as he picked up the box of books.

Hannah replaced the picture with the others. She was still curious about them, wondering who it was who had painted them.

"But dae ye know nothin' about the woman? Who is she?" she asked, but Hamish shrugged his shoulders.

"I don't know. I'd never seen them before. I don't even know who the artist is. Anyway, we should keep going. It looks like it's about to rain," he said, glancing up at the sky.

Clouds were gathering on the horizon, and rain was threatening as they hurried along the moorland path towards the croft. Maeve and Caitlin were playing outside, and they came hurrying to greet them, accompanied by Sheppey, who jumped up at Hannah and barked.

"Is Mother at home?" Hannah asked, and Maeve nodded.

"Aye, but we were sent outside – Uncle Brendan flew into a terrible rage with Mother and Aunt Rose. I've never seen him so angry," Maeve replied.

Hannah sighed. Her uncle's condition would not improve. He

needed to accept that and stop being so angry with those around him. Her aunt did everything for him, and still, he did not appreciate her or Hannah's mother.

"Come on, we'll go back inside. There's somethin' I need to speak to Mother about," Hannah said.

Hamish lingered outside, kneeling, and stroking Sheppey as Hannah followed Maeve and Caitlin into the croft, still carrying the box with the paintings in it. The atmosphere was sullen. The curtain was pulled across the alcove where her uncle slept, and her aunt was sitting by the fire darning socks. She did not look up as Hannah entered the house, but Hannah's mother was stoking the fire, and she turned to Hannah with a smile.

"Yer back, then?" she said, and Hannah nodded, setting the box down on the table in the centre of the room.

"Mother, there's somethin' I want to ask ye," she said, feeling suddenly nervous at the thought of her mother refusing the request she was about to make.

Hamish had nowhere else to go. He could not live in the hayloft at Balmoral, and if her mother refused, Hannah did not know where he could go.

"What's in that box?" Hannah's mother asked, as her aunt now looked up from her darning.

"It's Hamish, Mother–nae in the box, I mean… these are Hamish's things. He's outside now. He's had some terrible news. It's his uncle. He's dead," Hannah said, and her mother clasped her hands to her face and uttered an exclamation of horror.

"Dead? Oh, the poor lad. Left with nothin' and now to lose his uncle, too," she said, and Hannah nodded.

"Mother, he's got naywhere to go, could he… I mean, would ye let him stay here?" Hannah asked.

She held her breath, fearing her mother's response, but to her surprise, her mother simply nodded and smiled.

"Aye, Hannah, he can stay here. We've room enough. The two of ye are friends, and I'd nae see the lad given over to poverty.

Bring him inside. I'll cut some bread. There's drippin' in the bowl—I know he likes it. Will ye make some tea, Rose? We'll take care of the lad," she said.

Hannah was surprised at the ease with which her mother had agreed to her request. She had thought there would be some resistance on her part—even anger. Her mother still blamed the Royal Family for the death of Hannah's father, but it seemed she was not about to extend that prejudice to a boy who had lost everything.

"Ye can come in," Hannah said, as she hurried outside to where Hamish was sitting on the bench at the front of the croft.

He looked up at her and smiled, and Sheppey barked happily.

"Do you really mean it?" he asked, and Hannah nodded.

"Aye, my mother says yer welcome to stay as long as ye need to," she replied, and Hamish breathed a sigh of relief.

He rose to his feet and followed Hannah inside, where Hannah's mother had placed a large plate of bread and dripping on the table, along with a pot of tea.

"I'll make some griddle scones, too," she said, putting down the jam pot next to where Hamish now sat and smiling at him.

"It's ever so kind of you, Mrs. McGinn," Hamish said, as Hannah poured him a cup of tea and Maeve and Caitlin came to sit at the table.

"We McGinns know what tis' like to lose everythin' we held dear. But we know what tis' like to look forward, too. Ye can stay here as long as ye need to, Hamish," she said, placing her hand on Hamish's shoulder.

He smiled at her, glancing at Hannah, who felt relieved and grateful to have finally done something to help Hamish, even as the future seemed uncertain.

"Thank you. Thank you, all," Hamish said, taking a deep breath, as it seemed he was now part of the family.

SIR GEOFFREY GRAY

*L*ife at the croft settled once again into a predictable routine. For the next few weeks, Hamish accompanied Connor each morning to their work in the stables.

He was a hard worker, and whilst he admitted he found it hard to be a servant in the house where he had once held such a lofty position, he was willing to work hard to help the family. He gave his wages to Hannah's mother, and with two incomes and the pension provided to Hannah's uncle by Prince Albert, life was somewhat easier for the family than it had been before.

Hannah continued to help her mother with her mending, and would walk for miles across the moorlands, always accompanied by Sheppey, delivering the mended garments to outlying crofts and farms.

"Ah, thank ye, Hannah," Mr. McSween said, as he opened his farmhouse door to Hannah on the first day of June.

"My mother said to tell ye, Mr. McSween–she mends clothes, but is nay miracle worker. She cannae magic cloth out of thin air. Yer trousers had more holes in them than a sieve," Hannah said, as she handed over a neatly folded set of garments.

The farmer roared with laughter, and Hannah, too, laughed, for she imitated her mother's voice as she spoke.

"Oh, Hannah, tis' a fine thing, indeed. But yer mother always works miracles mendin' my garments. I was amongst the thorn bushes, pullin' out a lamb that got trapped there. That's why they got so torn. But look, she mended them perfectly," the farmer replied, holding up the pair of breeches Hannah had referred to.

Hannah did not let him in on the secret that her mother had entirely replaced the two legs with new material and charged him only with the repair. He handed over the payment and walked with Hannah across the small yard at the front of the house to the gate, which commanded a long view of the moorlands down towards the castle.

"Tis' a beautiful day, Mr. McSween," Hannah said, and the farmer nodded.

"Aye, and I've more sheep to go chasin' after. Tell me, Hannah, how's our young aristocrat? How's Hamish?" he asked.

"He's fine, thank ye. He works in the stables and seems happy enough. He gives his wages to my mother, and she feeds him and gives him board. I like havin' him there. He's a dear friend to me," she said, and Mr. McSween smiled.

"Yer an old head on young shoulders, Hannah. But I suppose ye had to grow up fast, did nae ye?" he said,

Hannah smiled. The farmer was right. She *had* grown up fast, bearing responsibility from a young age. She understood what Hamish was going through and had done her best to support him in his grief – a grief she knew all too well.

"I hope… I hope he'll be all right," she said.

"He's got a good friend in ye, Hannah. It was an unexpected encounter ye first had, but sometimes, when we're thrown together with another — how different we appear — we find things in common. People are nae so different. Scratch the surface, and ye'll find the same flesh and bone," he said, and with that, he bid her good day.

Hannah pondered these words as she walked home that morning. The farmer was right. She and Hamish were not so different. He was a duke, but she did not think of him as such.

Out on the moorland, or sitting around the fire at night, such titles meant nothing. He was Hamish, and she was Hannah. Their circumstances were the same now. There was nothing different about them.

"But perhaps he'll leave one day," she thought to herself, and that pang of sorrow she had felt at the thought of him being sent away to school returned.

They had grown used to one another. Hannah was pleased to have him close, and on their long walks with Sheppey, they often talked about what the future would hold, even as it seemed filled with uncertainty.

But as she approached the croft, Hannah was surprised to see a horse tethered outside. They were not expecting visitors, and she hurried forward, fearing this uncertainty would bring with it bad news.

Maeve and Caitlin were playing outside, and they turned to look at Hannah, who stared at them questioningly.

"We were sent outside to play," Caitlin said.

"Why? Who's here?" Hannah asked.

"A man. He came to see Hamish," Maeve replied.

Hannah hurried to the door. She had a feeling something was wrong, and as she entered the croft; she came face to face with a tall man, dressed in a long black cloak, riding breeches, and a top hat he had not bothered to remove.

He was wearing a white shirt with a tall, stiff collar at the neck, around which was tied a blue cravat, and he turned to look at Hannah with disdain. Hamish was there, along with the others, and was looking worried.

"Hannah, this is Sir…" Hannah's mother began, but she was interrupted by the man, who spoke with a pointed English accent.

"Sir Geoffrey Gray, cousin twice removed of the late Duke of Braemar. Hamish's only surviving relative. And you must be Hannah McGinn. I've heard a great deal about you," he said, though he did not elaborate further on whether those things were good or bad.

"I… I see," Hannah replied, though she did not understand why this distant relative should be standing in their parlour.

"Sir Geoffrey's come with news, Hannah," her mother said, and Hannah looked at Hamish fearfully.

He was looking worried, and Sir Geoffrey now placed his hand firmly on Hamish's shoulder.

"I've come to tell Hamish of his good fortune. His uncle didn't leave him entirely bereft. He's fortunate to have a distant relative–myself–of some import. I wouldn't see the boy left in such… unfortunate circumstances," he said, glancing around disdainfully at the croft.

"But I…" Hamish began, but he was silenced by the gentleman's interruption.

"The Duke of Braemar can't live under such conditions. He needs proper schooling and a to lead a life worthy of a gentleman. Working in the stables of Balmoral and living in a hovel such as this is no position or place for a boy of such rank. He'll come with me," Sir Geoffrey said, even as Hamish began to protest.

"But I… I don't know you. My uncle never mentioned you," he said, staring frantically at Hannah, who was terrified at the prospect of what was now going to happen.

Would Hamish be taken away from her? Tears welled up in her eyes, and she shook her head, even as Sir Geoffrey brought out a set of documents from his pocket.

"It's all here, and very clear. You can see from this correspondence with your uncle's lawyer – everything's above board. I'm not trying to steal from you, Hamish. You've got nothing of any value to your name. But as your closest living relative, it's my duty to do what I can to help you. I'm going to send you to school and raise you as a gentleman. You'll sign over your few possessions to me as your ward, of course. But it's all here–a legal document, given over by your uncle's lawyers. He wanted to provide for you, Hamish. And if he'd not been so foolish with his money, then perhaps there might have been something for you to have," Sir Geoffrey said, shaking his head.

The documents were spread out on the table. Hamish had been teaching Hannah to read, but the words were so complicated and the language of a legal and technical nature.

None of the others could understand it either, for their own reading and writing was limited. Hamish scrutinised the documents, shaking his head even as Sir Geoffrey tutted.

"But I... I don't want to go. I'm happy here," Hamish said.

"How can you be happy here? It's not in your best interests to remain here, Hamish. You can't stay here. You need a proper education. That's what I'm offering you. The chance for future happiness. You won't find it in a croft on a moor, or in the stables of Balmoral. I only wish I'd learned of your plight sooner. Did your uncle leave you anything... particular?" he asked.

Hamish shook his head.

"There wasn't anything left, just a few books, a couple of boxes, that's all," he said.

"And you still have these?" Sir Geoffrey asked.

"Sir, I think ye need to let Hamish think this over," Hannah's mother said, and Sir Geoffrey looked up at her in surprise, as though he had not expected her to have an opinion on the matter.

"And why, madam, would he need to think it over?" he asked, his voice dripping with contempt.

"Because he's been through a lot, that's why. He's lost his uncle, his home, his wealth–everythin' he held dear. And now ye come along and..." Hannah's mother began, but Sir Geoffrey interrupted her–he seemed adept at interrupting people.

"And offer him a future far better than any you could provide. I won't see him dragged down to your level, madam. I won't have the Duke of Braemar living in this... filthy croft, eking out an existence as a stable hand on the royal estate. It just won't do," he exclaimed, even as Hannah's mother bristled with anger.

"The only thing makin' this croft filthy are yer ridin' boots, sir. Now, I would ask ye to leave my home, and let Hamish decide for himself," she said, drawing herself up and pointing towards the door.

Sir Geoffrey laughed.

"There's nothing for him to think about. He's going to Gordonstoun. The arrangements are made. There's just the matter of his few possessions, and then we'll leave. I'll return in the morning," Sir Geoffrey replied, and before a retort could be made, he strode out of the croft, encountering Sheppey, who barked angrily at him.

As the sounds of horse's hooves disappeared into the distance, Hannah brushed a tear from her eye, shaking her head as Hamish looked down at the documents strewn across the kitchen table.

"I'd never heard of him before today. He arrived earlier, telling your mother his name, and waiting for me to return from the stables. I can't believe it. I don't want to go. But... do I have a choice?" he said.

Hannah glanced at her mother, who looked forlorn. It was a terrible situation, one which would surely only bring Hamish fresh misery.

"But why would yer uncle never have mentioned him? Is he really who he says he is?" she asked.

Hamish handed Hannah a card – it had Sir Geoffrey's details on it, and an address in London's Mayfair.

"He's left his credentials, and these documents relate our connection. He's a second cousin of my uncle, and that means he's related to me, too. I can only think my uncle forgot about him. But I don't see what he stands to gain from me. I've got nothing, and even after schooling. I'll have nothing," Hamish said, sitting down at the table with a sigh.

"He seemed very interested in yer possessions, Hamish," Hannah's aunt said, glancing nervously at Hannah's mother, who nodded.

"Aye, a box of books and a few portraits. Tis' hardly a king's ransom," she said.

"I don't even know where they are. I put them in the roof space a few weeks ago. They can stay there for all I care," Hamish said, glancing at the ladder which led up to the roof space above the croft.

"Perhaps he thinks ye've got a fortune, though," Hannah said.

She felt suspicious of Sir Geoffrey. He had appeared out of nowhere and seemed overly intent of controlling every aspect of Hamish's future. He was to be sent away to school, and then…

"But I haven't got a fortune. He must surely know that. He knows my uncle lost everything. There's only the title – no house, no estate, no fortune. It's all gone, lost on the gambling table," Hamish said, and he put his head in his hands as Hannah came to sit next to him.

"Ye daenae have to go with him," she said, even as she feared Hamish had no choice but to do so.

"But what if he's right? I don't mean about the croft and the work in the stables. I mean about me – I'm the Duke of Braemar. I might be penniless, but it means something. I can't just cast off my responsibilities–whatever they might be. No, I've got to go, I've got to do what my uncle would want me to do," he said, and he banged his fist down angrily on the table.

Tears rolled down Hannah's cheeks. She did not want to lose him, and now her mother gave a weak smiled and sighed.

"Ye've got to dae what's right for ye, Hamish. We cannae decide that for ye. Ye've been welcome in our croft, and we've been glad to have ye here. But if this is what yer uncle wanted for ye, then so be it," she said.

Hamish nodded. He looked at Hannah with a sorrowful look.

"I can write to you every week, every day, if you want me to. I won't forget you, I promise," he said, and Hannah forced a smile to her face.

"I should hope nae," she said, and he laughed.

"And you can write back and tell me about all the things you're doing. You can tell me about the professor, and Sheppey, and Mr. McSween. And I'll be back. But perhaps if I go now, I might come back as something more than a groom. I don't mean that to sound disdainful, but I'm not very good at it. I wasn't raised to be a groom. I was raised to be the Duke of Braemar. That's what my uncle wanted, and if Sir Geoffrey intends to make me so, then… I feel I've got to accept," he said, glancing again at the pile of documents on the table in front of him.

Hannah nodded. She understood, even as it upset her to do so. She had not wanted to believe he would ever leave. But despite their many similarities, Hannah and Hamish were different.

They were cut from different cloth, and Hannah knew their futures lay along different paths. She pulled out her handkerchief and dabbed at her eyes.

"I just… did nae think it would be so soon," she said, trying stop herself from crying any more, even as it felt her whole world was about to end.

A SAD FAREWELL

"I've spread some slices of bread with drippin' and wrapped them in muslin for ye. Ye'll be hungry on the journey," Hannah's mother said.

It was the next morning, and the family were preparing to bid Hamish farewell as they awaited the arrival of Sir Geoffrey.

"That's very kind of you, thank you. I won't ever forget your kindness to me. I'm only sorry to be leaving now," Hamish said, stowing the wrapped pieces of bread and dripping into his pocket.

Hannah was surprised to see tears in her mother's eyes, even as the sound of horse's hooves announced the arrival of Sir Geoffrey. Sheppey had been tied up, but he began to bark ferociously as a loud knock came at the door of the croft.

Hannah's mother went to open it, and Hamish's distant relative entered, surveying the scene with disdain.

"Are you ready, Hamish?" he asked.

Hamish stepped forward and nodded.

"I am, sir. I've read through the documents you provided, but you should know this—my uncle left me with nothing. I've no fortune, no house, no estate. Only my title, and the few clothes I stand up in. If you intend to educate me, you do so entirely at your own expense. I see no gain in your intentions—not for you, at least," he replied.

Sir Geoffrey's eyes narrowed, and he shook his head.

"I'm aware of your reduced circumstances, Hamish. I know there's no fortune. But a dukedom shouldn't disappear into obscurity, lost on a lonely moorland. What I do, I do for your sake, and the sake of the family to which I belong. I haven't asked you for anything, but I've promised you a great deal. Now, come along. You've got your possessions packed, have you?" he asked.

Hamish nodded, even as his possessions amount to only a small bag and nothing more. The books and paintings remained in the roof space above the croft, packed behind several trunks containing clothes and rugs for the winter.

"I don't have anything but what you see me with now," Hamish replied.

Sir Geoffrey looked at him curiously.

"Weren't there some books? A few odds and ends?" he asked, but Hamish shook his head.

"Nothing, sir. Only what you see me with," he replied.

Hamish had confided in Hannah his intention not to mention the paintings. He did not know why, but he was suspicious of Sir Geoffrey's motives, and wanted to test him by presenting himself as completely penniless.

His relative nodded, appearing unconcerned, even as he glanced suspiciously around. What we he looking for? Hamish had come there with nothing. His uncle had left him destitute. He had no money, and no possessions except for the paintings and box of books.

"Very well. You'll come with me now. We leave for Gordonstoun immediately," Sir Geoffrey said, beckoning Hamish to follow him.

Hannah was determined not to cry. She did not want to appear weak in front of Sir Geoffrey, and along with the others, she followed him and Hamish outside. Sheppey was barking, and Hamish leaned down and ruffled the dog's ears.

"It's all right, boy. I'll be back. I promise," he said, glancing up at Hannah. As if his words of reassurance were really meant for her.

"You'll have no reason to return here," Sir Geoffrey said, and Hamish turned to him and shook his head.

"You don't understand. You think I've been unhappy here? I haven't. I've been happier here than I ever was anywhere else in England. When I came from India with Mimi, I thought I'd never be happy again. And when my uncle died… I didn't know where I'd go or what I'd do. But these people took me in. They gave me a home, and they showed me what it was to be loved," he said.

Hannah could not hold back the tears she had forbidden herself from crying, and they ran down her cheeks, as she shook her head and stepped forward.

"I daenae want ye to go," she exclaimed, catching him by the arm.

He, too, had tears in his eyes, and he gazed lovingly at her, even as the pain of separation seemed to overwhelm them both.

"It's not forever, Hannah," he whispered.

She reached into her pocket and brought out the case with the butterfly in it. It was her most treasured possession, and now she thrust it into his hands. He looked down at it in astonishment.

"But… you can't give me this, Hannah. It's precious to you," he said, but she shook her head.

"If ye have it, it means ye'll come back. I'm nae givin' it to ye. I'm lendin' it to ye. Think of me when ye open it," she said, and he nodded.

"I will do," he said, as Sir Geoffrey gave an impatient snort.

"Come along. The carriage awaits. We leave for Gordonstoun as soon as we get off this godforsaken moor," he said, and Hannah now watched as Hamish followed him to the tethering post, and they both climbed up onto the waiting horse.

Hamish raised his hand, waving to the family, who stood at the door of the croft.

"I'll miss him," Maeve said, slipping her hand into Hannah's.

"And I'll miss him, too," Hannah replied as tears rolled down her cheeks, and the horse carrying Hamish and Sir Geoffrey disappeared over the brow of the hill towards Balmoral.

Hannah stood watching as her aunt and sisters returned inside. Connor was at work in the stables, and her uncle was still in bed, so that now she was left standing next to her mother.

"Why were ye cryin' when Hamish left, Mother?" she asked, and her mother shook her head, fighting back her emotions.

"Because… he reminds me of ye, Hannah. And it felt as though I were seein' off my own child, nae a stranger's," she said, shaking her head as she put her arm around Hannah and held her close.

"I'm goin' to miss him so much, Mother," Hannah said, sobbing into her mother's shoulder and clinging to her as she wept.

"I know, Hannah. But… perhaps he was only meant to teach ye the first lesson," her mother replied, and Hannah looked up at her, confused as to what she should mean.

"I… I daenae know what ye mean," she replied.

"We all must lose someone we love, Hannah. Tis' the sorrow of life. To love and lose. Love comes and goes. We find the one to love us in return, and they stay awhile. But tis' better to have loved and lost than never to have loved at all. Ye've been taught that lesson early, and perhaps tis' a blessin' rather than a curse," her mother said, leading Hannah to sit down on the bench by the window.

They sat in silence for a few moments, looking out over the moorland. Hannah rested her head on her mother's shoulder, no longer sobbing, but thinking about her mother's words.

She *was* in love with Hamish, even as she did not entirely understand what that meant. She knew she missed him terribly and wanted him only to return. But was her mother, right? Had she lost her first love? Would she ever see him again?

"But... he promised he'd come back," she said, and her mother smiled at her and ran her hand through her hair.

"And how many poor souls have waited on that promise, Hannah? Perhaps he will, and perhaps he will nae. But daenae upset yerself. Ye've shared somethin' special together. He's made ye happy. He's brought us all a little happiness, and I hope we've brought him some, too," Hannah's mother replied.

"And have ye changed yer mind about aristocrats?" Hannah asked.

She had been surprised at the way in which her mother had treated Hamish. She had expected her to treat him with the contempt she reserved for the Queen and the Royal Family. But the opposite had been true.

For the short time Hamish had been with them, Hannah's mother had treated him as the son she had never had, and now it seemed she missed him in just the same way, too.

"I... I held onto that bitterness for too long, Hannah. I blamed everyone I could for yer father's death. But what good did it dae me? I was none the happier, was I? He's dead, and I will nae bring him back by blamin' the likes of Hamish, will I? Nay, Hannah. I have nae changed my mind about aristocrats, but some are better than others," she replied, and kissing Hannah on the top of her head, she rose to her feet and returned into the croft.

Hannah could hear her telling Maeve and Caitlin to tidy their clothes up and help with the mending, but Hannah sat for a while on the bench, looking out over the moors. She thought of Hamish, wondering what he was thinking.

He had been sad to leave–that much was certain. But was her mother, right? Would he forget her? Sheppey came and rested his head on her knee. She smiled down at him and fondled his ears.

"Yer a faithful friend, Sheppey," she said, and the dog yelped and pawed at her.

He wanted to go for a walk, and with her mind still filled with thoughts of Hamish, Hannah rose to her feet and called for the dog to follow her. They set off up the mountain path, making in the direction of the professor's croft.

Hannah could see for many miles across the glen, and she looked down at the turrets of Balmoral, shaking her head at the thought of what the Royal Family had brought to this lonely part of Scotland.

When Hannah was born, the moorland had been a remote and lonely spot, but the coming of royalty had changed that forever, and so much of her life–whether by intention or chance–was bound up with their arrival.

"Good day, Hannah. And what brings ye to my door today?" the professor said, waving to her as Hannah came to the croft, with Sheppey racing ahead.

The professor and the dog were firm friends now, and Sheppey jumped into the professor's lap and stretched out his paws. The professor laughed and began rubbing Sheppey's stomach.

"Hamish left, Professor," Hannah said, and the professor looked at her in surprise.

Left? What dae ye mean? Where did he go? He had naywhere to go," the professor replied, and Hannah sat down with a sigh and recounted the story of Sir Geoffrey and the promise of an education for Hamish.

After Hannah had finished her explanation, the professor shook his head and sighed.

"And I daenae know if I'll ever see him again," she said, fighting back the tears.

"We always see our friends again, Hannah–if tis' meant to be. He will nae forget ye," the professor said, but Hannah was not convinced.

She feared Gordonstoun would be the end of their friendship. Hamish would be with boys of his own kind. He would be taught how to be a duke, and that would mean forgetting life on the moors.

"But I fear he will, Professor. I daenae know… will ye help me write letters to him?" she asked, for she feared her own abilities at writing would fall far short of Hamish's letters to her – if they even arrived.

"I will, Hannah. But dae I forget ye when I go back to Edinburgh? Nay, I daenae forget ye. I often sit in my study at the university and think of my friend in the highlands. I wonder what yer doin' and where yer goin'–just because I'm far away, doesnae mean we're nae friend, does it?" he said.

Hannah shook her head. The professor was right. They did not see one another for most of the year, and yet when he returned each year, it was like they simply picked up the conversation where they had left off. She thought about him, too, and thinking of Hamish in a similar way was enough to cheer her a little.

"Yer right, Professor, I'll see him again, just… nae as much as I thought I would," she said, and the professor smiled.

"We can write him a letter in the next week or so and tell him about Sheppey's adventures on the moor. Shall we take him for a walk now?" he asked, smiling at Hannah, who nodded.

The professor held out his hand, and Hannah took it, looking at Sheppey as the dog leaped up at her excitedly.

"Come along, Sheppey. Tis' time for a walk," she said, and the dog barked.

"He's seen a butterfly. Look, there it goes," the professor said, pointing across the heathers to where a butterfly fluttered in the breeze.

They hurried after it, and Hannah laughed at the sight of the professor, as excited as a child at the prospect of a sighting. They followed the butterfly across the moor, until at last it settled on a large gorse bush, where, to Hannah's astonishment, hundreds of others were gathered.

Reds, orange, yellows, greens, blues, indigos, and violets – every shade imaginable, of every colour Hannah could think of. It was remarkable, and she stared at the gorse bush in amazement as the professor clapped his hands together in delight.

"But Professor... have ye ever seen anythin' like it?" Hannah asked, and the professor shook his head, kneeling in the heathers and staring up at the butterfly covered gorse in delight.

"Tis' a gatherin' – I've heard of such things. The warm breeze brings them together. But to see one. Tis' a blessed day, Hannah," he said, inviting her to sit next to him, as together they marvelled at the sight of hundreds of butterflies, all dancing on the gorse bush.

Sheppey, too, appeared mesmerized by the sight, and sat next to Hannah, staring up with wide-eyed admiration.

"I can tell Hamish about this in my first letter. He'll be amazed to hear about it," Hannah said, and the professor nodded.

"Aye, Hannah. And perhaps we'll all three return to the gorse bush and see this sight again. Sheppey knows the way well enough," the professor said, patting the dog on the head.

Sheppey rolled onto his back, wagging his tail, but Hannah could not tear herself away from the sight of the butterflies, a reminder of how beauty can spring from the most unlikely of places–the caterpillar bursting forth, and creating the spectacle before them.

She thought of Hamish, and whilst she was sad to see him go, she felt certain he would not forget her, just as she vowed never to forget him, either.

PART III

THE BRAEMAR PORTRAITS

Spring 1859

"Another bag of mendin'–tis' the sorry lot of a seamstress. The work's never done," Hannah's mother said, sighing as she heaved the bag of clothes onto the table and tipped it out.

There were shirts, breeches, an overcoat, and dozens of pairs of socks, all worn and torn. Hannah shook her head and smiled.

"Aye, Mother, but if there were nay clothes to mend, there'd be nay bread on the table, either," she said, and her mother nodded.

"Aye, tis' true enough," she said, picking up a dirty shirt and holding it up to the light.

It was summer on the moorlands, and Hannah had just turned eighteen – her birthday being in July. The past few years had passed by with predictable regularity, and the day was like any other.

Hannah helped her mother around the croft, whilst her aunt took care of her uncle, who was now permanently bedridden. They took in mending, and Hannah and her mother would sit for many hours, stitching and darning the torn clothes of their neighbours, who kept them supplied with a steady stream of work.

"I must have repaired this shirt of Mr. McSween a dozen times. It'll be a new shirt before long. I'll have to patch the side. Look at this tear," Hannah said, holding up the shirt for her mother to see.

Her mother shook her head and laughed.

"Well, as ye say, Hannah–if he keeps tearin' them, we keep mendin' them, and the bread stays on the table. Tis' only fortunate yer sisters are provided for now. Times are getting' harder," she said, shaking her head.

Hannah nodded. Her two sisters–Maeve and Caitlin – worked as maids at "the big house." Balmoral Castle was finished, a spectacular sight from the hills surrounding it, and flying the royal standard, as the Queen and Prince Albert–the Prince Consort as he was now known–were currently in residence.

"Perhaps we'll be sent some of the royal linens to repair," Hannah said, and her mother laughed.

"I'd make a hole in them deliberately. And I doubt Her Majesty has her clothes repaired. If she tears a piece of lace or a silk shawl, she'll simply demand a new one. Nay, Hannah, we'll nae be getting' anythin' sent from the royal household. They have ladies in waitin' to see to all that. I think of Maeve and Caitlin down there… why did they go and work there?" she said, shaking her head.

Hannah knew she should not have mentioned the Royal Family. Her mother's heart was still set against them, and she took any opportunity to speak ill of them.

Maeve and Caitlin had done well–Maeve was a chambermaid, whilst Caitlin was second maid to Her Majesty's dresser, a position which could lead to considerable progression in the royal household.

"Because tis' a better life than mendin' shirts, Mother," Hannah replied.

She did not mean to sound resentful, but there were days when Hannah despaired as to her future. She loved her mother dearly, but her life seemed to stretch before her without purpose, mending other people's clothes, and eking out an existence at the croft – it was hardly the life she had aspired to, even as she had not known to what she should aspire.

Such thoughts had been weighing heavily on her in the past few months, but one glimmer of hope remained–her monthly letter from Hamish.

"And what's wrong with mendin' shirts? Was it nae good enough for me and my mother before her?" Hannah's mother demanded, and Hannah sighed.

"I'm sorry, Mother. Tis' just… well, I have nae heard from Hamish in a while," she said, glancing at the door, as though she imagined his once familiar knock to sound in that moment.

In the six years since Hamish had been sent away to school, Hannah had only seen him once. But they had written to one another every month.

The professor had helped Hannah with her reading and writing, and now she could write to Hamish without the help of the kindly academic, who still came to stay at the croft on the mountainside above and spend his summers searching for butterflies.

"Ye had a letter from him last month, did nae ye?" her mother asked.

"Aye, but I wrote back, and I have nae heard from him since. He was sent to London – some further schoolin' after Gordonstoun, but… I daenae know," Hannah replied, sighing, and shaking her head.

She and Hamish lived such different lives, and as they grew older, it seemed as though those lives were heading in very different directions. Hamish had completed his studies at Gordonstoun at the expense of Sir Geoffrey, his benefactor, and a man who maintained an iron grip over him.

He had been sent to London, and was pursuing studies in the

legal profession, even as he had written to Hannah and told her how much he detested such work.

"It's so dull, Hannah. I think of the moorlands every day, of running across them in pursuit of the stag. I think of the two of us together, and of the freedom we enjoyed. How I long for what you have," he had written.

Hannah felt the same. She longed to be with him, even as she knew it was an impossibility. He was the Duke of Braemar, and she was the mere daughter of a highlander, a crofter without prospects.

It was foolish to imagine anything more, and Hannah had long since resigned herself to a parting of ways. Whatever Hamish said, their destinies were very different.

"Write to him again. I'm sure ye'll hear from him. Ye always dae," her mother said, taking up her darning and shaking her head.

Hannah returned to her own mending, lost in thoughts of the past. She missed Hamish terribly. Absence had made her heart long for him, even as she told herself to think of a different future if she was ever to find the happiness she longed for.

* * *

MAEVE AND CAITLIN were due to return home for their day off later that afternoon, and Hannah's mother had been busy baking in expectation. They had one day off a week, which they took together, walking back to the croft from the castle.

Hannah always looked forward to her sisters' day off and would go to meet them on the moorland path, excited to hear their news of the world inside the castle, where the Royal Family lived in splendour. A world away from that of Hannah and her family.

"Yer a little late today," Hannah said, as her two sisters came into view along the path.

"Tis' a busy time at the castle, Hannah. Her majesty's hostin' all manner of important people to a dinner this evenin'–we were all kept busy," Maeve said, greeting Hannah with a kiss.

"I was allowed to lay out Her Majesty's silks–her gloves, and a shawl. I had to place them on the dressin' table just so. She was in the next room. My hands were tremblin' terribly," Caitlin said, and Hannah smiled.

"We were just talkin' about Her Majesty. I said to Mother, I wonder if we'd ever be sent any royal linens to repair," Hannah replied, and Caitlin laughed.

"Oh, nay, Hannah. Her Majesty would never have anythin' repaired. If there's a tear–or even a thread out of place – the lady in waitin' or Her Majesty's dresser discards it. She has so many beautiful things. Ye should see the number of trunks which arrived from London," Caitlin said, shaking her head.

The three sisters walked arm in arm towards the croft, and as they approached, Sheppey came running to greet them. He had taken to sitting outside in the summer, basking in the sunshine, or chasing butterflies–something the professor strongly disapproved of. Now, he leaped up at the three sisters, barking excitedly.

"If there's one person who's always pleased to see ye, it's Sheppey. He's never down, never in a bad mood, and always with a smile on his face," Maeve said as she fondled the dog's ears.

"Dog's daenae smile," Hannah said, laughing at her sister, who blushed.

"I think Sheppey does. He certainly seems happy to see us," Maeve replied.

"Aye, that's because ye bring him bones from the royal table. He's practically nobility," Hannah said, as Caitlin opened the basket she was carrying and took out a large bone, which she presented to Sheppey with great ceremony.

"Yer Majesty," she said, bowing, as all three of the sisters laughed.

Sheppey took the bone with similar ceremony, laying it down on the ground and sniffing it.

"Tis' beef, Sheppey–from the banquet last night. I'm sure ye'll like it," Caitlin said, and now Sheppey settled down to gnaw at it.

"Ye spoil him," Hannah said, shaking her head.

"Oh, I nearly forget. There's a letter for ye, Hannah. I think it's from Hamish. It was delivered to the castle," Caitlin exclaimed, rummaging in her basket once more and bringing out an envelope.

Hannah let out an exclamation of delight and snatched the letter from her sister's hand. Hamish often sent his letters to the castle for her sisters to deliver. A prominent address like that was far more likely to find a way for delivery than a remote croft on the moorland above.

"We'll go in and see Mother," Maeve said, as Hannah opened the letter and sat down on the bench outside the croft.

It was written in Hamish's familiar handwriting, and as she read, Hannah could hear his voice, as though he was sitting opposite her, speaking the words on the page.

"My dear Hannah, forgive me for the delay in replying to your letter of last month. It found me in the middle of another set of exams. My benefactor remains determined for me to have a legal education, even as I cannot, for the life of me, understand why I need one. I was pleased to read of the professor's return. I know the two of you are the greatest of friends. But I want to share some good news with you, too–I am coming back to Balmoral," Hannah read.

At these words, she gasped, and a tear rolled down her cheek. She had seen Hamish last when he was sixteen–and only for a few brief moments. He had been summoned to Balmoral for the reading of his uncle's will, a document which had been discovered by his benefactor, quite by chance.

It had left everything to Sir Geoffrey, and its circumstances were suspect, even as Hamish had found no grounds to challenge it. He was provided for by means of his benefactor and having

THE CROFTER'S DAUGHTER

lost his entire fortune on the gambling table, Hamish's uncle had little to leave him.

At that time, Hamish had paid the briefest of visits to the croft, and he and Hannah had walked together across the moorland with Sheppey. All too soon, Hamish had left, and Hannah had imagined she might never see him again.

"But now he's coming back," she said to herself, as she continued to read.

"I write these words to you in confidence. My benefactor does not yet know of my plans. But I am of age now, and my schooling is complete. I miss the moorlands, the glens, the mountains – I miss you, too, Hannah. I shall return in the coming months and come at once to the croft to see you. There is much to tell you about, but in person, not by written word. I think of you every day, Hannah, and to be with you again–and to see Sheppey, of course–will be a dream come true. I remain, ever yours, Hamish."

Hannah smiled, reading through the letter a second time, and pinching herself to prove she was not dreaming. To think of Hamish returning to Balmoral filled her with joy, and she wondered how soon it would be before that familiar knock came at the door.

"Hannah, are ye comin' in for tea? Mother's made griddle cakes," Caitlin said, opening the window and leaning out.

Hannah turned to her and smiled.

"Aye, I'm comin'–I've just had the most wonderful news, Caitlin. Hamish is comin' home," she said.

* * *

TALK at the table that afternoon was entirely about Hamish's return. The whole family was excited, and Hannah's mother promised to invite him for tea.

"I've never known anyone to enjoy bread and drippin' more

than the Duke of Braemar," she said, shaking her head and laughing.

"I daenae ever think of him as a duke. I wonder what he's like now. Will he have airs and graces to him, dae ye think?" Caitlin asked.

"Airs and graces? Yer the one layin' out silk gloves and a shawl for Her Majesty," Hannah replied, and Caitlin laughed.

"Aye… but that's different. She's the Queen. But Hamish… he lost everythin' did nae he? Tis' so sad to think… but now he's comin' back, and… ye must be so happy, Hannah," she said.

Hannah nodded. She had missed Hamish dreadfully, and to think of him returning home was a balm to all her troubles. But she, too, feared the passage of time may have changed him.

Would he still be the same Hamish who had left her all those years ago? Their lives were so different, and yet by accident they had become entwined. She read through his letter once again, smiling at the thought of seeing him very soon.

"We still have those old boxes up in the roof space. The books and portraits," Hannah's aunt said.

"He'll nae want those," Hannah said, for she had not given the boxes a second thought since they had been put there all those years ago.

"He might dae. Wait until Connor comes home. He can lift them down for ye," her aunt replied.

"Tis' only a few boxes, Aunt Rose. We can manage," Maeve said, and before Hannah could stop them, her two sisters had climbed up into the roof space to retrieve the boxes, sending down a shower of dust and debris as they did so.

"I just swept the floor. Ye'll get dust everywhere," Hannah's mother exclaimed, as Maeve and Caitlin climbed down from the roof space, covered in dust, and with the boxes triumphantly in hand.

"There, now. Here they are," Maeve said, setting the boxes

down on the table, another cloud of dust erupting from them as Caitlin opened them.

Hannah sneezed and peered inside. The books were damp and mouldy, but the set of six paintings were still in excellent condition. The study of a pretty young woman with a pale face and large, blue eyes. Her hair was short and drawn back. Her lips were bright red, and she wore a starched collar, laced, and secured at the neck with a ruby red brooch.

Hannah looked at her, wondering who she was. She remembered seeing the portraits for the first time and asking the same question. Caitlin was looking at them curiously, and now she frowned, as though trying to remember something.

"What's wrong?" Hannah asked.

"Well… I'm nae sure. But these were Hamish's pictures?" she asked, and Hannah nodded.

"Aye, they were sent from Braemar on the day the news of his uncle's death arrived. We brought them back here when Hamish came to stay with us. They've been up there ever since," Hannah replied, pointing towards the roof space.

"What's wrong, Caitlin?" Maeve asked, and Caitlin blushed.

"Well… I shouldnae betray Her Majesty's confidence, but when I was layin' out the gloves and shawl, I overheard her talkin' to Prince Albert. The door was closed between the dressin' room and the bedroom, but they were talkin' about a set of portraits. Six portraits of a woman. They called them the Braemar pictures. Her Majesty said they're worth a fortune – the most expensive portraits in all of Scotland. But nay one knows where they are," Caitlin said.

Hannah looked down at the paintings. There were six of them. They depicted a woman, and they had come from the Braemar estate. No one could know they had been stowed away in the roof space of a remote highland croft ever since the death of Hamish's uncle. And now she stared at them in astonishment.

"Dae ye think… but nay, it cannae be. The Duke of Braemar

CATHARINE DOBBS

was left with nothin' when he died. Hamish had nothin' – but perhaps… well, if nay one realised their worth at the time," Hannah said, staring at her sisters in amazement.

"But that's what Her Majesty said. They were lost for centuries. They're late medieval. But there's a record of them havin' been at the Braemar estate. If Hamish's uncle knew the truth about them, perhaps he made sure to hand them onto Hamish. Perhaps he's nae poor at all. He's the Duke of Braemar. They belong to him, and if they're as valuable as the Queen said they were… well, his troubles are over," Caitlin exclaimed.

Hannah shook her head. It was a remarkable possibility, even as she could hardly believe it to be true.

"But dae ye really think they could be the portraits?" Hannah asked.

"There's only one way to be certain. We take them to Balmoral and ask. The equerry could show them to Her Majesty," Caitlin replied, but Hannah shook her head.

"Nay, they belong to Hamish. It's him who must decide what to dae with them. I'll write to him. But we should keep them hidden for now. Tell nay one," she said, glancing from Maeve to Caitlin and back.

"But why?" Caitlin asked.

Hannah was thinking back to the arrival of Sir Geoffrey– Hamish's benefactor. She had not thought much of it at the time, but now she remembered his persistence when it came to establishing those things which belonged to Hamish.

He had asked specifically about Hamish's possessions, even as the new duke had remained somewhat vague about what precisely his uncle had left him.

"Because of Sir Geoffrey–Hamish's benefactor. Daenae ye remember how interested he was in Hamish's possessions? And turning up so unexpectedly, and just at the right time, too. There was somethin' suspicious about him. Perhaps he knew about the portraits and was lookin' for them. Dae ye remember when

Hamish came back for the readin' of his uncle's will? There was somethin' suspicious about that, too. But it makes sense now," Hannah said, staring down at the portraits and shaking her head.

She had disliked Sir Geoffrey, even as she had put his behaviour down to that of an arrogant aristocrat. But the discovery of the paintings now made her think again.

If these pictures were the most valuable in all of Scotland, then it was no wonder Hamish's supposed benefactor had been so eager to discover the duke's inherited possessions.

"Then what are we to dae with them? We daenae even know if these are the pictures the Queen was speakin' of," Caitlin said, in a tone which suggested she rather regretted relaying the conversation she had overheard.

"We keep them hidden. I'll write to Hamish and tell him we've found… somethin' of interest. I will nae tell him what. When he comes, he can decide," she said.

The others looked at one another with anxious expressions on their faces.

"But is it dangerous to keep them?" Hannah's mother asked, but Hannah shook her head.

"Nay one knows we have them here, dae they? Tis' a secret, and only discovered by chance. They've been safe here until now. We'll put them back in the roof space and wait until Hamish returns," she said.

Another cloud of dust ensued as Caitlin and Maeve hauled the boxes up the rickety ladder and hid them in the roof space. Hannah was trembling with excitement, and she sat down immediately to write to Hamish about the news of their discovery, choosing her words carefully.

"Dae ye think he'll be pleased?" Maeve asked, as she sat watching Hannah write.

"Aye, if they're truly the Braemar pictures, he will. He's got nothin' to call his own but sellin' such a set of portraits would restore his fortune. Tis' nay wonder his benefactor wanted to get his hands on them," Hannah said, shaking her head.

She tried to imagine Hamish's reaction. He would surely be delighted to learn of the possibility, even as Hannah remained uncertain why he was returning to Balmoral.

His letter spoke of missing her, words she echoed in her reply, but despite his sentiment, Hannah knew there was nothing at Balmoral for a penniless duke. She had no doubt of Sir Geoffrey's intentions, even as she wondered how Hamish could ever escape his grasp.

"Come back soon," she concluded, sealing the letter and imagining the moment when Hamish's knock came at the door.

INTERESTING NEWS

⚜

Hannah had no qualms in taking the professor into her confidence over the portraits. She visited him the following day, finding him reading a book in the sunshine. As Sheppey raced up to him, barking loudly, the professor looked up at and smiled.

"Ah, Hannah, did ye know a butterfly's wings ae transparent? The colour makes them appear as they they're nae, but they are," he said.

Hannah smiled back at him. He always had something interesting to say, but today, she was pleased to have something interesting to tell him, too.

"I've got a secret, Professor. But ye must solemnly swear to tell nay one," she said.

The professor sat up in his chair and looked at her with interest. He put his hand on his heart and drew in a deep breath.

"I solemnly swear–unless yer in danger, Hannah. I cannae promise faithfulness then," he said, but Hannah shook her head.

"Nay, nae danger… but, tis' a risk," she replied, and now she proceeded to explain the arrival of Hamish's letter and what her sister had overheard in the royal dressing room about the forgotten paintings.

The professor listened with interest, nodding, and fixing her with a searching gaze.

"And ye truly believe these are the Braemar portraits?" he asked.

"I daenae know, but I've written to Hamish and told him..." she began, but the professor gasped.

"Did ye tell him ye had them? What if his benefactor sees the letter?" he exclaimed, but Hannah shook her head.

"Nay, Professor. I told him... well, I told him there was somethin' he needed to see at the croft. I told him to come at once when he returns," Hannah said, blushing at the thought of the words she had used.

She had told Hamish how much she missed him, and how she had thought of him every day since last, they had seen one another. His own letter had been so filled with affection, and Hannah wanted only to share with him her feelings as to his return. The professor nodded.

"Aye, tis' well ye did. If that letter falls into the wrong hands... still, nay one would suspect the portraits are where they are. Tis' a remarkable discovery. I've heard of them, but they're presumed lost. The newspapers in Edinburgh were full of the story when I left. Tis' some ancient document recently discovered relatin' to the Braemar estate. It speaks of the six portraits–a Lady Isabella Braemar, a Spanish princess who came to Scotland to marry the first duke. The portraits were a study–done in Spain–and sent for the duke's approval. He fell in love with her as soon as he set eyes on her. Tis' a remarkable story. But the portraits were presumed lost, until now," he said, smiling at Hannah, who could hardly believe what she was hearing.

"She's very beautiful," she replied, thinking back to the paintings.

There was no doubt in Hannah's mind–they had found the

Braemar portraits, and that would surely mean the restoration of Hamish's fortune. She was excited at the prospect of Hamish's return and was now awaiting a response to her letter.

She had sent it with Caitlin to the castle, where it could easily be posted. That had been three days ago, and Hannah felt certain she would receive a swift reply.

"I'd like to see the portraits for myself. But they should stay hidden until Hamish returns. Daenae show them to anyone, Hannah. And if anyone comes askin' for them, tell them ye know nothin' of them," the professor said.

Hannah nodded. She had no intention of showing the paintings to anyone, and she had sworn her sisters – and Connor to — secret. Even Mr. McSween had not been told of the discovery, despite commenting on the amount of dust on the floor of the croft when he had visited Hannah's uncle with some home-brewed ale the day before.

"I'll keep the secret safe, I promise. But if they're the portraits, what happens then?" Hannah asked.

"Hamish can reclaim his rightful place in society. He'll have nay need of his benefactor–if, indeed, Sir Geoffrey really is his benefactor. There's somethin' suspicious there, Hannah. After everythin' ye've told me about him... aye, be careful," the professor said.

They spent a happy hour together discussing the species of butterflies the professor had catalogued since his arrival on the moors that summer, including one he still could not identify.

"But ye know every butterfly in the world, Professor," Hannah said, and the professor laughed.

"Nay, Hannah–tis' the joy of my science. Butterflies inhabit the whole world, but to be an expert on them all... nay, tis' nae possible. A man in Scotland can know his own butterflies, whilst a man in South Africa can know his. I'd be lost there, and he'd be lost here. Nay, I need to think more about the colours I saw–

CATHARINE DOBBS

perhaps tis' a new breed, unknown to our collections. But I'll catch it," he said, tapping his nose.

Hannah's stomach was rumbling as she made her way down the mountain path with Sheppey back towards her mother's croft. The sun was warm on her face, and a pleasant breeze carried with it the scent of the heathers.

She paused, watching as her cousin came along the moorland path from the direction of Balmoral. She waved to him, and he beckoned her to come to him.

"There's a telegram for ye, Hannah," he said, handing her a folded piece of paper from his pocket.

Hannah looked at him in surprise. She had never received a telegram before and did not really understand what one was.

"A telegram?" she said, unfolding the piece of paper.

It was short. Neatly transcribed in black ink.

"Take precaution. Stop. Coming soon. Stop. Others searching. Stop. Hide findings. Stop. Hamish," she read, furrowing her brow in confusion.

"It arrived earlier today. The equerry brought it out to me. He was nae very pleased. He said telegrams shouldnae be delivered to Balmoral for crofters," Connor said, shaking his head.

But Hannah cared nothing for the equerry's sensibilities. Her heart was racing as she read through the telegram once again. Hamish's words–exaggerated by the style of communication– were clear.

Danger hung over them, and the portraits were the object of the duke's fears. Hannah had chosen her words carefully in her letter, never mentioning the paintings, but referring to the books and "other items" which Hamish had inherited.

It was clear he had heard about the paintings and had made the connection between what was hidden in the roof space of the croft and his own seemingly worthless inheritance.

"We need to be careful, Connor. Does anyone else know

about the telegram?" Hannah asked, fearing the equerry's anger may have led to his revealing the contents to others.

"Well… I daenae know. But the telegrams arrive throughout the day. They're usually for the Queen or Prince Consort or their guests. That's why this was so unusual. I suppose anyone could've seen it, though," Connor replied.

"Did anyone ask ye about it?" Hannah asked, her beating fast, but Connor shook his head.

"Nay one asked about it. I brought it straight back with me. But what does it mean?" he asked, looking confused.

"It means we have to be very careful," Hannah replied with a grim expression on her face.

* * *

FOR THE REST of the day, Hannah was restless. She was waiting for Hamish, even as his telegram had given no indication of when he would arrive. She ate no dinner, and her mother chastised her for pushing her stew around her dish instead of eating it.

"What's wrong with ye, Hannah?" she asked, as Hannah set down her spoon with a sigh.

"Tis' Hamish's telegram, Mother. I daenae know when he'll be comin' back. The portraits—they must be those everyone's lookin' for," she said, sighing and sitting back from the table.

"And all ye can dae is wait for Hamish to return, Hannah. When he does, ye'll know more," her mother replied, shaking her head.

She was right, even as Hannah continued to feel anxious. She kept glancing up to the roof space, imagining the paintings being discovered at any moment. What would happen if the Queen found out the truth?

"Aye, Mother. I know. I just wish… oh, I daenae know. I daenae even know him dae I? Nae really," Hannah exclaimed.

That was her true worry—not the paintings—but Hamish

himself. They had seen one another only once in the past six years, and only for a fleeting time. Their letters were filled with warmth and affection, but as for knowing Hamish as he now was… Hannah was fearful.

She imagined him as he was when they were younger, not now, not after he had finished his education and been sent to London for further studies. Their lives were so different, and whilst Hannah longed to see him, she could not imagine they would still have anything in common.

Her two sisters looked at her anxiously, and her mother shook her head and tutted.

"People change, Hannah. Ye cannae prevent it. But tis' nae for ye to say what Hamish will or will nae be like. Perhaps he thinks the same of ye. Have nae ye changed since last ye saw him?" she asked.

Hannah nodded. Her mother was right. Change was inevitable. They had both changed, grown up, moved in different directions. Neither of them had stayed the same, and Hamish was surely thinking the same of her as she was thinking of him.

Their meeting had been entirely by chance – the accident involving Mimi and the pony bringing them together in the most unexpected of circumstances. Theirs was a friendship which never should have been, even as it had come to mean everything to Hannah.

"I suppose so… well, yes, I have. It's just… well, I daenae know what to say to him. Tis' goin' to be a strange thing when he knocks at the door," Hannah said, and her mother smiled at her.

"Aye, well, ye'll be pleased to see him when he does, Hannah. Think how ye've agonised over his return. And now he's about to come back, yer anxious to see him," her mother said, shaking her head.

Hannah smiled and nodded. Her mother was right. She *had* waited for this moment. She had longed for it. But now it seemed fraught with danger, a danger Hannah could only imagine the consequences of.

She was curious about the paintings, and fearful, too. If they were truly the lost Braemar portraits, what would happen then? She had so many questions, even as she knew she must be patient and wait.

Her sisters were at work at Balmoral, and Connor had to return to the stables later that afternoon – several gentlemen were to ride out to hunt the following day, and Connor had work to do.

Hannah helped her mother clear away the dinner things, and with her uncle fast asleep and her aunt sitting at his side with her embroidery, Hannah sat with her mother by the fire, continuing the mending they had begun earlier that day.

"I dae want to see him–Hamish, I mean. But… well, tis' a worry, still," she said, and her mother smiled.

"Oh, Hannah, ye poor lass. Yer still in love with Hamish, I can see that," her mother said, and Hannah blushed.

She had not realised it was so obvious, even as she knew there could surely be no doubt as to her feelings for the duke, whose torch she had held ever since he had left for Gordonstoun.

"I just… well, yes, I am," she admitted, and her mother patted her hand.

"But ye cannae live yer whole life in love with him, Hannah. Tis' nay good. He cannae love ye back, ye know that," she said, with a sad look on her face.

Hannah knew this, too. A duke did not marry a crofter– however close they had become. He would be expected to marry according to his station in life — the daughter of an aristocrat, or even one of the royal princesses.

If the Braemar paintings were proved real and Hamish's fortune was restored, he would take his rightful place in society and marry whomsoever he chose.

When Hamish had been as poor as she, Hannah had imagined

CATHARINE DOBBS

the possibility of their being together–of marrying and raising a family. It had all seemed so simple once, the two of them chasing across the moorland together, following the deer with Sheppey.

Nothing else had seemed to matter in those moments, but with title and wealth came responsibility, of which Hannah was all too aware.

"But I think he does love me, Mother. Why would he write every month if he were nae in love with me?" Hannah replied.

Her mother sighed and shook her head.

"Perhaps he clings to the past, too. But there're other possibilities, Hannah. Ye will nae have to stay here darnin' socks with yer mother yer whole life long," she said, and Hannah smiled.

She felt guilty for what she had said to her mother, even as she had meant it at the time.

"I did nae mean to say those things, Mother. I like helpin' ye darn socks," Hannah replied, but her mother only laughed and shook her head.

"Ye dae right to want somethin' more for yerself, Hannah," she replied.

Hannah was about to answer when a loud knock at the door brought her back to her senses.

She leaped to her feet, her heart beating fast–this was surely Hamish returned, and hurrying to answer, she flung open the door with a smile on her face. But it was not Hamish who appeared before her, and she stared in astonishment as Sir Geoffrey Gray glared back at her.

"Well, young lady, we meet again," he said, pushing past her into the croft.

AN UNWELCOME VISITOR

Hannah's mother looked up in surprise, and her aunt rose to her feet as Sir Geoffrey strode into the croft and pulled out a chair at the table.

"Ye cannae just burst in here like this," Hannah's mother exclaimed, looking angrily at Sir Geoffrey, who waved his hand dismissively.

"Sit down, Hannah. I want to talk to you," he said, as Hannah closed the door and sat back down next to her mother.

The early evening sunshine was coming through the window, and it fell on the benefactor's pale face, extenuating his bone structure and making him look somewhat otherworldly as he held a silver topped cane in his right hand.

"I don't understand. Has something happened? Is it Hamish?" Hannah asked, thinking perhaps Sir Geoffrey had come to deliver unwelcome news.

But the benefactor shook his head and fixed Hannah with a searching gaze.

"It's not Hamish, no, Hannah, but I'm curious about something. I understand he's returning to Balmoral. I knew nothing of the matter until my arrival here this morning. Tell me, did he give a reason for his intended return?" he asked.

Hannah was confused. She had assumed Sir Geoffrey knew of Hamish's planned return to Scotland, but it seemed she had known long before his benefactor had discovered the facts–if indeed he was meant to have done.

"I… ye assume I know he's returning," Hannah replied.

Her response was quick-witted. Sir Geoffrey had tried to catch her out, and now she fixed him with a confused expression, even as he scowled back at her.

"But you did know. He sent a telegram to you. The equerry told me it arrived this morning. What did it say?" he asked.

Hannah was about to respond, but it was her mother who replied.

"Telegram? Really, Sir Geoffrey. Dae ye think we receive such things up here in this lonely spot? A telegram. Pray–where would a telegram come from to be delivered here?" she asked.

Hamish's benefactor looked annoyed, scowling at Hannah's mother and shaking his head.

"You received a telegram from Hamish today. I want to know what it said. Your cousin brought it," he replied, banging his fist down on the table in frustration.

"Oh, ye mean Connor. He's nae here now. Ye and yer party of gentleman are takin' up his night. He's got to get the horses ready for the hunt tomorrow. If there's a telegram, it'll be with him," Hannah said, and Sir Geoffrey scowled at her.

He was silent for a moment, running his tongue over his lips before narrowing his eyes and fixing Hannah with a searching look.

"In his letters… did he mention anything about his possessions? The things he brought with him from the Braemar estate, things of value?" the benefactor asked.

Hannah shook her head.

"Nay, Sir Geoffrey. There was nothin' he brought. His uncle

left him penniless. I thought that's why ye paid for his schoolin'– he had nothin' but the clothes he stood up in. That's all," she replied.

Hannah knew Sir Geoffrey could not be certain Hannah had ever seen the Braemar paintings, nor could he be certain they were hidden in the croft. He was acting only on a hunch, one which Hannah was determined to resist. Sir Geoffrey held her gaze, as though daring her to lose her nerve.

"No... paintings? I ask because it seems there's been a theft at some point in the years past. Some paintings... of inconsequential value, but of sentimental worth, are missing. I'd like them back – as part of the late duke's legacy," he said, glancing around him, as though he expected to see the paintings hanging on the nearest wall.

"And ye think we'd have such pictures on our walls, Sir Geoffrey? We crofters barely have enough to eat – let alone the money to buy pretty portraits," Hannah's mother exclaimed.

"And Hamish made no mention of these paintings in his letters to you?" the benefactor persisted.

"I daenae know anythin' about any pictures, Sir Geoffrey," Hannah said, and the tone of her voice caused Sheppey to bark emphatically.

Hamish's benefactor scowled once again, rising to his feet and bashing the tip of the silver topped cane on the floorboards three times.

"I know you're lying. You know more about this than you're letting on. I'll be remaining at Balmoral for some time, and If Hamish is returning, I'll be waiting to greet him. And don't think I won't be watching you–all of you," he said, glancing around the room.

"Get out of this croft," Hannah's uncle shouted, but Sir Geoffrey only laughed.

"A cripple telling me what to do–now there's an amusement. Perhaps I'll tell His Royal Highness to stop your pension.

Harbouring paintings that don't belong to you, conspiring to defraud a friend of the Royal Family. I'll see to it you don't last long in this croft, sir," he snarled, as Hannah's mother sprang towards him.

"Get out! Get out! I'll throw ye out," she exclaimed.

The force and swiftness of her action took Sir Geoffrey by surprise, and he stumbled backwards, falling into the door, as Sheppey barked and worried at his ankles.

He scrambled to his feet, striking out at the dog with his cane. Sheppey yelped, retreating under the table, as Hannah, too, lunged forward. She struck Sir Geoffrey across the cheek–as much for Hamish as herself.

"Ye heard my mother and my uncle–get out of this croft," she exclaimed, and pulling open the door, Sir Geoffrey hurried out, cursing them under his breath.

Hannah breathed a sigh of relief, leaning back against the door, as her mother went to look out of the window.

"He's gone," she said, shaking her head.

"But he'll be back," Hannah's uncle said, and Hannah glanced fearfully at her mother, who shook her head.

"Let him try. He's a wicked man. I feel so sorry for Hamish. A fine benefactor he's turned out to be–he's only interested in one thing. Those portraits, and what they're worth to him. He'd have taken them if Hannah had told him they were here," Hannah's mother said, still watching from the window.

Hannah went to join her. She could see Sir Geoffrey's horse disappearing along the moorland path, and she wondered how long it would be before he returned. She glanced anxiously at her mother.

"He did nae believe us, did he?" she asked.

"But he cannae say why. He's lyin'–there's nay sentimental value attached to them. He wants to sell them for his own gain. He's nothin' but a wicked aristocrat. They're all the same," her mother exclaimed.

"Except Hamish," Hannah replied.

She was glad she had kept Hamish's secret, even as she feared it could not remain a secret for long. She was anxious for him to return to Balmoral.

It was a burden she was finding hard to bear alone, particularly now her family was involved, too. There was no telling what Sir Geoffrey was capable of – his threats could so easily come true. And without her uncle's pension, the family would be left destitute.

"Hamish still needs to prove himself, Hannah. I daenae know what'll become of us… tis' a dreadful worry," her mother said, glancing up towards the ladder leading to the roof space, as though she imagined the paintings to be mocking her.

Hannah sighed and glanced out of the window.

"Where are ye, Hamish?" she asked herself.

* * *

But Hannah did not have to wait long for news of Hamish's return to reach her. It was Maeve and Caitlin who brought it. They arrived from Balmoral the following afternoon, informing Hannah that a carriage bearing the Duke of Braemar had just arrived as they were leaving for their evening off.

The Queen herself had received her Godson in the drawing room, accompanied by Sir Geoffrey Gray, and Hannah set off at once, hoping to meet Hamish as he walked up the moorland path.

"Make sure he takes responsibility for the portraits, Hannah," her mother said, fixing Hannah with a stern expression as she left.

"I will dae, Mother. But there're still so many unanswered questions," Hannah replied.

She set off along the moorland path, followed by Sheppey who, it seemed, had sensed the return of his master. As she walked, Hannah wondered what she would say. It had been so long since the two of them had seen one another.

There was so much she wanted to say, even as she knew she would struggle to find the words to say it. The paintings were foremost on her mind, as was the visit of Sir Geoffrey to the croft the evening before.

It had unsettled her, and Hannah had passed a restless night, every sound giving way to visions of an assault on the croft in search of the portraits.

"It'll be all right," she told herself, as she made her way down the winding path through the trees towards the castle. It was as she was approaching the lawns; she saw him.

He was taller than before, and his face was that of a youth now growing into a man. Hannah was surprised. She knew he would have changed, but seeing him so was still a shock. She waited for him at the edge of the trees, smiling at him as he approached.

He was holding a single rose–a red rose, plucked from the gardens–and he smiled back at her, handing her the rose before taking her by the hand and raising it to his lips.

"I'm so glad to see you. I thought you might come. I was about to walk up to the croft. And here's Sheppey, too. Good boy," Hamish said, ruffling the dog's ears, as Sheppey barked and jumped up at him,

"We've both missed ye," Hannah said, and Hamish laughed.

"Not as much as I've missed the two of you. They weren't expecting me at Balmoral. Sir Geoffrey's terribly angry about it all. But I wasn't intending to stay there. I was going to walk up and ask the professor if I could stay with him. It's all a dreadful mess, Hannah. But you've not said anything, have you?" he asked, suddenly becoming serious.

He glanced over his shoulder towards the castle, as though he was expecting to have been followed.

"Sir Geoffrey came to the croft last night," Hannah said, and Hamish stared at her in surprise.

"He came to the croft? Are you alright? Did he threaten you?" he asked, and Hannah nodded.

"He's convinced we're hidin' the portraits—which we are. But I still daenae understand, Hamish. Are they the Braemar portraits?" she asked, and she explained how Caitlin had overheard the conversation between the Queen and Prince Albert, and how she had become convinced the six paintings were those they had spoken of.

They walked up the forest path whilst she talked, and Hamish nodded, his face grave.

"It's true. I hadn't thought about them for years. But it was Sir Geoffrey who brought up the topic. He'd read about the portraits in one of the newspapers—some uncovering of a medieval manuscript. The Braemar estate is sold, of course, and the new owner—the one who took it from my uncle—discovered the paintings were missing, and their worth. Now, his claim on them is null and void. The sale of the house paid the debts—that's all settled. But the whereabouts of the paintings remained a mystery. Until now," he said, shaking his head.

"But Sir Geoffrey believes ye have them?" Hannah asked.

"He does, yes. He believes it. He had my rooms in London searched, and the cellars of Gordonstoun, too. There's no way of proving it, but I know it was him. His visit to you only adds to the evidence against him. He wants those portraits for himself. They're definitely the ones. The manuscript details them—six paintings of the Spanish princess who married the first duke. They're by a Spanish artist—Felize San Delaccio. His work adorns the churches of Spain, and when he wasn't painting religious imagery, he painted royalty instead. They're worth a fortune, Hannah," Hamish replied.

Hannah was astonished. The paintings had been hidden for six years in the roof space of the croft—a fortune sitting right above them. It was too incredible for words, and Hannah shook her head, pausing to catch her breath.

"But what now? They're yer paintings by all rights, but what can ye dae to claim the fortune? Ye'll sell them, will nae ye?" she asked, and Hamish nodded.

"I'll sell them to my godmother. They'd be the highlight of the royal collection. But I've no doubt Sir Geoffrey would challenge me. I remain his ward–at least for now. He's threatened me, of course. But I'm convinced he's really nothing to do with my uncle. I've been looking into it, you see–he wasn't ever listed amongst the family members, and I can't find any trace of him in any official documents relating to the family. He claims to be a distant cousin, but it's all nonsense, of course. Nevertheless, he's a dangerous man," Hamish replied.

They had come to the moorland path now, and Hamish paused, turning to Hannah and smiling.

"I'm worried–I'm scared," she said, voicing her fear for the first time.

He slipped his hand into hers and squeezed it.

"I'm sorry, Hannah. We've talked of nothing but the paintings since we met. I meant it when I said how much I'd missed you," he said, and Hannah gave a weak smile.

"I've missed ye, too–with all my heart," she replied, and tears welled up in her eyes.

"I had to come back. I hated London. Studying law–it was nonsense. I'm the Duke of Braemar. What do I need to know about such things? When I heard about the paintings, well... I remembered the box in the roof space above the croft. I'd have thrown those old portraits away if it weren't for you. Now, I realise my uncle might have known the truth as to their value. He lost everything, but he made sure he did something for me in return. He left the paintings, hoping one day I'd realize what they were worth – why he never told me, I don't know. Or perhaps they weren't worth anything at all to him, and all this is just fate.

But don't worry. None of that matters. I'm just glad to be here with you," he said, squeezing her hand.

They sat down on a bank of heather, looking out across the moorlands, the royal standard fluttering above the castle below. It felt to Hannah as though no time at all had passed since the last time they had been together, even as it felt like a lifetime, too.

"I thought perhaps ye might forget me, Hamish–first at Gordonstoun, then in London," she said, and he turned to her and smiled.

"How could I forget you and all the adventures we had? Didn't I write to you every month without fail?" he said, and Hannah nodded.

"Aye, I know. I'm just bein' foolish, that's all. But when I read yer letters, I read of a different world, so far from my own as to seem like a dream. The places ye described, the people ye met, the things ye did–they were all so different from life on the moorland. I never knew what to say to ye. I was darnin' socks and chasin' Sheppey across the heathers. Tis' the life I was born into, the only life I've ever known. But yer life…" she said, shaking her head as her words trailed off.

"I wanted my life to be like yours. Free from expectations. To come and go as I pleased. I loved to hear about your walks with Sheppey and your visits to the professor. Don't you realize that?" he asked, and Hannah smiled.

"Aye… tis' hard to imagine, though," she replied, feeling suddenly shy.

He shook his head and smiled back at her.

"You should imagine it. Receiving your letters was always the best moment of my time at school. I used to imagine you out here on the moors with Sheppey or sitting at home in the croft with your mother and sisters or visiting the professor. I wanted to be there. I wanted to do those things… with you," he said.

Hannah could not understand why such mundane things should attract him. How often she herself had imagined his life as her own, for despite his hardships, he had still enjoyed a privilege the likes of she could only dream of.

"And I wanted to be with ye, too. I thought of all the things ye told me about–lavish dinners, playing sport, weekends in the countryside at the homes of yer school friends. I couldnae imagine what those things were like," she said, shaking her head.

He smiled at her and laughed.

"Interminably boring. I hated every moment of it. It was Sir Geoffrey who forced the issue. I was expected to do this and that–to be seen. I'm the Duke of Braemar, or so he kept reminding me. But I'll show him–I won't let this rest. I'm going to sell those paintings. He won't get his hands on them. He keeps telling me he saved me–but from what? All of this? I'd gladly have remained here my whole life long. I could've been a crofter or a gillie," Hamish said.

Hannah laughed. She remembered Hamish's stalking skills – they were rather like his uncle's, and more likely to scare away the herd than come to a point where it could be hunted.

"Ye still could. Why dae as Sir Geoffrey tells ye? Challenge him," Hannah said, and Hamish nodded.

"I intend to. There was nothing I could do before–I was his ward, but now… I understand things much better now. But I want to see the paintings, though. I need to be certain," Hamish said, and offering Hannah his arm, the two of them made their way along the moorland path towards the croft, with Sheppey running happily at their feet.

* * *

Hannah's mother was standing outside the croft, hanging washing on the line, and she paused as Hannah and Hamish approached, greeting the duke with a smile.

"So, the wanderer returns. Nay longer a lad, but a man," she said, and Hamish smiled.

"I hope I've grown up a little, Mrs. McGinn," he said, as Caitlin and Maeve came out to greet him.

"We brought the news ye'd arrived," Maeve said.

"Ah, yes, the two maids. It's wonderful to see you. How do you find life at the castle?" he asked.

Maeve and Caitlin exchanged glances.

"Tis' pleasant enough, though Her Majesty can be demandin' at times," Caitlin said.

At these words, Hamish laughed.

"I know that well enough. She demanded my presence earlier today. Being the Queen's godson has its advantages, but it comes at a price," he replied, as they stepped inside the croft.

Hannah's uncle was fast asleep on the bed, and Connor was at work in the stables, but Hannah's aunt greeted Hamish warmly. Her mother hastily cut several slices of bread, which she spread liberally with drippings and placed in front of Hamish on a large plate, whilst Hannah made the tea.

"I know ye like bread and drippin's—more than dainty sandwiches," Hannah's mother said, and Hamish grinned at her.

"You know me too well, Mrs. McGinn," he said, glancing at Hannah, who knew what he wanted to see.

"Caitlin? Maeve? Will ye get the box of pictures down from the roof space?" she asked.

"I've just swept the floor," her mother exclaimed, but she made no further protests, and midst a cloud of dust, the paintings were brought down.

Hamish pushed aside the plate of bread and dripping, and lifted each of the paintings out, placing them side by side on the table. His eyes grew wide as he looked at them, shaking his head as though in disbelief.

"I can hardly believe it. These are the paintings. There's no doubt about it. I've read about the study, and there're sketches of the paintings in the documents attesting to them. I remember them hanging on the wall of my uncle's library, but I never gave them a second glance. They were just a set of paintings amongst all the others," he said, picking up the nearest and holding it up to the light coming through the window.

"And yer certain these are the ones?" Hannah asked.

"Oh, quite certain. And I want to thank you all for keeping them hidden all this time," he said, and Hannah smiled, even as she felt nervous at the thought of knowing the paintings were really those worth a fortune – the Braemar paintings the Queen herself had spoken of.

"And to think we've had them here all this time," Hannah's mother exclaimed.

"And to think I nearly told you to burn them for fuel for the fire," Hamish replied, shaking his head in astonishment.

"Then yer fortune's restored, Hamish. Ye daenae need Sir Geoffrey anymore. He wanted them for himself. Tis' all clear now," Hannah said, glancing towards the door as though she expected Sir Geoffrey to burst through at any moment.

It was the most remarkable discovery, and Hannah's heart was beating fast at the prospect of what it meant.

Hamish was no longer poor. He could be the Duke of Braemar now. There was nothing to stand in his way. He had wealth befitting his rank and could claim all things which were his privilege.

"That's right, and we've all the proof we need now. I doubt he's got any connection to my family – none whatsoever. He's a con artist of the highest order. But we'll show him, Hannah – only when the time's right, though," Hamish replied.

"But we should hide the portraits again. Nay one knows for certain they're here. But if Sir Geffrey found out…" Hannah said, feeling suddenly fearful of what Hamish's benefactor was capable of.

"You're right. Until he's exposed, anything could happen. Let's put them back in the roof space until the right time. It's given me such a thrill to see them," he said, and Hannah smiled.

"I'm just glad they're the pictures ye believed them to be," she said, and Hamish nodded.

"And it's all thanks to you and your family, Hannah," he replied.

Hannah blushed. She would gladly have done it again, even as she feared losing him for a second time.

She wondered what would happen when the matter was resolved and the paintings were sold – surely a duke would not wish to reside in the lowly dwelling of a crofter, when he had a fortune to his name. She knew her thoughts were idle, even as she allowed her mind to linger on them.

"We were only too glad to help ye," she replied.

"But where are ye stayin' tonight, Hamish? Ye cannae go back to the castle, surely," Hannah's mother said, and Hamish shook his head.

"I'll sleep out on the moors. It's a fine night, and I've dreamed of doing so during my long months in London," he said, but Hannah's mother shook her head.

"I'll nae hear of it. Ye can sleep in the bed with Connor. Ye'll catch yer death of cold out on the moor. The days may be warm, but the nights are cold," she said, and there was no argument Hamish could give to persuade her otherwise.

Hannah made a stew for dinner, and baked potatoes in the embers of the fire. As darkness fell, her mother lit the lamps around the walls, and a pleasant atmosphere descended on the croft. Hamish regaled them with tales of his school days at Gordonstoun, and his life in London.

"I've never been to a big city before. I cannae imagine what tis' like," Caitlin said, looking fearful at Hamish's descriptions of busy thoroughfares and towering buildings.

"You get used to after a while. It doesn't hold any fear for me. But I missed the wide-open spaces of the moorlands, and the fresh air of the mountains. London's a dirty place. It's hard to breathe sometimes," Hamish replied.

"But ye wouldnae want to go back there?" Hannah asked.

She did not yet fully understand Hamish's intentions. Would he leave Balmoral behind after the paintings were sold? He had spoken of how much he had missed her, but she felt unsure as to what this really meant.

Did he love her, or had he simply clung to a past which had never really presented the possibility for anything more than friendship?

"Not if I can help it. I don't want to go anywhere. I want to stay here – not at Balmoral, but… well, if I have the money, I can do as I please. I can help you all," he said, and Hannah looked at him in surprise.

This was the first time he had spoken in such terms, and she glanced at her mother, who smiled.

"Ye cannae stay on a lonely moorland, Hamish. Yer future lies elsewhere," she said, but Hamish was adamant, shaking his head as he fixed Hannah with a resolute gaze.

"I don't want to it to live elsewhere. I may be the Duke of Braemar, but that doesn't mean I want to be an aristocrat. I saw what such a life did to my uncle, and it's not the life I want for myself. Look at the like of Sir Geoffrey. Would anyone want to be like him? No, money can change a person, but it won't change me. I belong here. At least, that's how I feel," he said, and Hannah smiled.

She wanted him to remain–she wanted him to feel he belonged with them. His was a world she did not understand, a world she did not want to understand. Her own life was simple. It was nothing like his, and yet fate had brought them together in the most wonderful of ways.

"You should stay with us, Hamish," she said, and Hamish smiled.

"I intend to–and if these paintings are worth what they're claimed to be, then I can help you all, including your uncle," he said, glancing towards the bed where Hannah's uncle lay sleeping.

Hannah's aunt looked at him in astonishment.

"Dae ye mean it? The operation?" she said, and Hamish nodded.

"We can go to London–or Edinburgh. He'll receive the finest care money can buy. But that all lies ahead of us," he said, yawning as he spoke.

It was growing late, and when Connor returned home from his work in the stables, he was surprised to find another occupant in his bed.

"Tis' only for a few nights, Connor," Hannah's mother said, even as Connor laughed.

"I could've stayed down at Balmoral and slept in the stables with the horses," he said.

But it was all in good humour, and soon the croft was quiet. Hannah shared a bed with her two sisters when they were not at the castle, whilst her mother slept on a mattress on the floor next to the bed occupied by her aunt and uncle. Hannah found it hard to go to sleep that night, mulling over all that had happened and all that was to come.

"He says he'll stay, but will he, really?" she wondered.

There was nothing for Hamish on the moorland or the croft. A duke could not be a gillie or a beater his whole life long. She pondered this, listening to the sounds of her uncle snoring.

It was late now, and she was restless, unable to sleep, even as her eyes were heavy. Sheppey was sleeping on her feet–just as he did every night–but suddenly he looked up, cocking his head and growling.

"Sheppey?" Hannah whispered, as a sudden noise outside disturbed the silence of the night.

Hannah thought she could hear footsteps and low voices. She sat up and shook Maeve awake.

"What... what's wrong?" Maeve asked, sleepily.

"Tis' a noise outside. Sheppey heard it, too," Hannah said, pulling back her blanket.

But as she did so, a banging came at the door, and the sound of a man's voice echoing through the night.

"You in there, open up in the name of Her Majesty," it called out.

The others now awoke, and Hannah could see the outline of Hamish emerge from behind the curtain where he and Connor were sleeping. Her cousin followed, and now her mother got up, too, hurrying to the door as the shout came again.

"Who are ye? What dae ye want?" Hannah's mother called out.

"Open up in the name of Her Majesty, or we'll break the door in," the voice replied.

"They've nay right to demand such a thing," Hannah's uncle exclaimed, sitting up in bed.

Her aunt had struck the tinder and flint, lighting a candle to illuminate the scene. Hannah looked fearfully at Hamish, who now stepped forward and cleared his throat.

"You out there, identify yourself. You're speaking to the Duke of Braemar, Godson to Her Majesty the Queen," he called out.

"I'm Lord Archibald Sloane. Open this door," the voice called back.

Hamish stepped forward, followed by Connor, the two of them glancing at one another, and Hamish now pulled back the bolt and opened the door.

Outside stood a short man, dressed in riding breeches, shirt, and waistcoat. His face was illuminated in the moonlight and he looked Hamish up and down with disdain.

"What's the meaning of this? You come here in the middle of the night, disturbing the peace. I've never heard of a Lord Archibald Sloane. What does my godmother want with this dwelling at such an hour?" Hamish demanded.

"I speak for Sir Geoffrey Gray, your benefactor. You're to

THE CROFTER'S DAUGHTER

return to Balmoral immediately," the man said, but Hamish only laughed.

"And on what authority does Sir Geoffrey speak? I doubt your title, sir, just as I doubt his, and…" Hamish began, but at that moment, Hannah let out a cry.

Smoke was billowing from above, and the crackle of fire could now be heard coming from the roof space. The roof of the croft was thatch and wattle, and a single spark could easily set it ablaze. Now the sound of horse's hooves was heard, and a horse and rider charged off across the moor.

"He's got the paintings," Hamish exclaimed, as Hannah realised with horror the distraction they had fallen for.

The man at the door had been a decoy, whilst another had climbed onto the roof and pulled away the thatch. Now they had the paintings, and the croft was alight!

GIVING CHASE

Hannah's mother screamed as the flames swept through the roof space and thick smoke billowed all around them. Hamish and Connor rushed to lift Hannah's uncle from the bed, whilst her mother and aunt shooed Caitlin and Maeve outside.

The man claiming to be Lord Archibald Sloane was gone, and as Hannah looked out across the moorland, she could see the rider racing across the heathers, carrying the paintings under his arm.

Turning, she saw the flames licking up over the roof of the croft, creating a beacon which was surely visible for miles around. Her mother was crying – this was their home, and without it, they would have nothing and nowhere to go.

"The paintings, Hannah," Hamish said, pointing across the heathers.

"We'll follow them," she said, filled with a sense of injustice and anger at what had happened.

"But they'll be impossible to find on this vast expanse of moorland," Hamish replied, shaking his head.

But Hannah took him by the hand, urging him to follow her.

THE CROFTER'S DAUGHTER

"They daenae know the moor like we dae. If we can stalk the deer, we can stalk a horse and rider," she replied.

The rest of the family were standing back, watching as the flames engulfed the croft. There was nothing they could do to put out the fire. The roof was almost gone, and now the side walls were beginning to collapse.

Hannah's mother was sobbing, and her uncle was sitting in the heather shaking his head, as Caitlin and Maeve comforted their aunt.

"Then let's follow them, then. Perhaps there's still a chance," Hamish said, and followed by Connor and Sheppey, they set out in pursuit of the thieves.

* * *

IT WAS STILL DARK, though the first light of dawn was breaking gradually on the far horizon. The sky was clear and starry, the moon hanging low and full above. The thief had made south, following the path which led towards the farm belonging to Mr. McSween.

"He'll have to follow the trail this way. He cannae go across the heathers," Hannah said, as they hurried along the path.

"But why? He could go anywhere," Hamish said, running alongside her as Sheppey barked at their heels.

"Because the ground is nae firm. There're quagmires all over, and any horse would soon flounder in the mud, or fall from the path – just like Mimi's pony," Hannah said.

She knew the moor better than anyone, and even as a small child, she had known not to leave the paths for fear of falling into deep mud. Her father had told her he had once seen three cattle flounder and sink, watching in desperation as they drowned in the mud.

The moorland was dangerous to the uninitiated, and as they ran on, Hannah hoped to use this knowledge to her advantage.

CATHARINE DOBBS

Looking back, she could see the flames from the croft, lighting up the early dawn, which glowed red in return. It brought tears to her eyes. It was the only home she had ever known, and now it had been taken from them, just as the fortune of the paintings, too, had been snatched away.

"Be careful, Hannah," Connor called out, as Hannah turned off the path.

"He went this way," she said, pausing at a point where the heathers were trampled.

"But that way leads to…" Connor began, looking fearful as his words trailed off.

"Aye, the quagmires – and that's where we'll catch him," Hannah replied.

She knew it was a terrible risk. A wrong step and they could find themselves knee deep in mud and sinking to their waists.

To be trapped in one of the quagmires without help would mean death, and as Hannah left the path, she did so with thoughts of her father's warnings foremost in mind. Hamish and Connor followed.

Their pace was slower now, and Hannah chose their route carefully. Testing the ground ahead, gently resting her foot down in case it should sink. The sun was rising now, and the dawn was breaking.

Hannah could see further ahead, and she paused, glancing around her across the moorland, now bathed in the red glow of the early morning sun.

"Can you see anything? Are you certain they went this way? I don't see how you can know," Hamish said, but Hannah nodded.

"I know they came this way. Look at the way the heather is here – flattened – and the marks in the mud. They're fresh. A horse rode this way today, and we can be certain it was the thief," she replied.

"But they'll be miles away now. We should go back and help the others," Connor said.

Sheppey barked, sniffing at the ground, and looking up at Hannah with an expectant gaze.

"Sheppey knows they came this way, too. Come on, we cannae go back now. There's nothin' to go back to," Hannah replied, and without waiting for an answer, she hurried on, followed by Hamish and Connor, with Sheppey racing ahead.

The quagmires would not swallow a dog. Sheppey was light of foot, and whilst Hannah had to test every step, the dog charged across the heathers, yelping and barking.

"He's found something," Hamish said, pointing towards Sheppey, who now stood at the top of a low ridge, barking loudly.

"Careful, there could be a quagmire here," Hannah said, catching hold of Hamish's arm, just as he was about to run forward.

She tested the ground in front, nodding as the tip of her toes sank into the mud.

"Is it dangerous?" Hamish asked, and Hannah nodded.

"If ye'd gone forward, ye'd have been up to yer waist. Come this way. Ye can see the firmer ground where the heather grows thicker," Hannah replied, and now they followed a circuitous route onto the ridge.

Sheppey was still there, barking, and now Hannah could see the object of his excitement.

Down below, a horse and two riders were floundering in the mud. They had become trapped in one of the quagmires, and whilst the horse was half in and half out, the two men were up to their chest, and fighting for their lives.

"Sir Geoffrey," Hamish exclaimed, and now Hannah recognised Hamish's benefactor, along with the man who had claimed to be Lord Archibald Sloane.

"We need to help them. Whatever they've done, nae man deserves to drown in the mud of a quagmire," Connor exclaimed, and the three of them made their way cautiously down the ridge towards the quagmire.

"Get us out of here, Hamish," Sir Geoffrey cried out, but Hamish shook his head.

"The paintings, Sir Geoffrey. Where are they?" he asked.

Hannah glanced around her, and now she saw the paintings lying scattered on the ground. They had been in a saddle bag, and she picked them up, handing them to Hamish, who breathed a sigh of relief.

"They're not damaged," he said.

"Get us out of here," Sir Geoffrey's companion cried out, struggling in the mud.

"Daenae try to move. The more ye struggle, the deeper ye'll go," Hannah called out.

The two men had sunk further into the mud, but to enter the quagmire would mean certain calamity for anyone else. Connor was helping the horse, who had managed to struggle onto firmer land.

"Help me, Hamish," he called out, and Hamish hurried to help him, even as Sir Geoffrey let out an angry cry.

"Leave the horse, help us," he exclaimed.

"Just as ye helped yerself to the pictures and burned our croft to the ground?" Hannah called back.

Sir Geoffrey scowled at her. But he was powerless to do anything but flounder in the mud, and Hannah knew they had him in their power.

"They're worth nothing, and the fire was an accident," Sir Geoffrey called back.

"We know they're the Braemar portraits, and we know ye want them for yerself. As for the fire – it was nay accident. Ye started it out of spite, ye wicked man," Hannah said, just as Hamish and Connor managed to free the horse, which dragged itself up onto firm ground, whinnying as the two men caught its reins and calmed it.

"One rescued – the innocent party. As for the others…"

Hamish said, but at that moment, a shout came from the ridge above.

Hannah looked up to see Mr. McSween, who now slid down the bank, a coil of rope slung over his shoulder.

"Yer mother told me ye'd gone after the thieves. I was worried one of the three of ye might get stuck in a quagmire. But I see tis' a different story to tell," he said, and Hannah smiled.

"Aye, Mr. McSween, but we could dae with yer rope," she replied, glancing back to where Sir Geoffrey and his companion were now up to their necks in mud.

"Ye could always let the mud go to their mouths – tis' nay less than they deserve," he said, but now he uncoiled the rope, and along with Hamish and Connor, the rescue was enacted.

First, they pulled Lord Archibald Sloane from the mud, dragging him onto dry ground, where he spluttered and coughed, rolling onto his back, as Hannah looked down at him and shook her head.

"Dae ye still act in the name of Her Majesty?" she asked, and the man scowled at her.

"How dare you speak to me like that," he snarled, but now Hamish seized him by the scruff of his neck and dragged him to his feet.

"Keep a civil tongue in your head. I'll make sure Her Majesty knows everything you've done," he said, as Mr. McSween threw the rope to Sir Geoffrey, whose chin was now touching the mud.

He grabbed hold of the rope, and Hamish, Mr. McSween, and Connor hauled him out of the quagmire with considerable effort. He emerged onto the firm ground, covered from head to toe in mud, and dripping wet. He spluttered, looking up at Hamish, who shook his head.

"I'm finished with you, Sir Geoffrey. I don't believe a word of what you say about being a distant relative of mine. You forged my uncle's will, and you'd have left me entirely destitute, stealing my inheritance and making me a pauper. Well… I see through you now, and you'll be brought to justice for what you've done," Hamish said as Sir Geoffrey looked up at him and scowled.

"The paintings, they belong to me," he exclaimed, but Hamish laughed.

"They don't belong to you at all. They belong to me, and now I know why my uncle left them to me. Everyone thought they were worthless, but you found out the truth, didn't you, Sir Geoffrey? That's why you were so keen to get your hands on them. The paintings belong to me, and so does the money I'll make from selling them," Hamish replied.

Sir Geoffrey cursed him, but there was nothing he could do, and now Mr. McSween pulled the muddy rope from the quagmire and smiled.

"Shall we leave them tied up here until the proper authorities arrive?" he said, with a glint in his eyes.

"How dare you," Sir Geoffrey exclaimed, staggering to his feet.

But he and Lord Archibald Sloane were no match for Hamish, Connor, and Mr. McSween. They were soon tied together, sitting back-to-back next to the quagmire, as now Hannah and Hamish turned their attentions to the paintings. Despite their adventure, they were each in perfect condition, and Hannah held one up, smiling at the sight of the now familiar Spanish princess.

"She's beautiful. I'd have loved to have met her," she said, and Hamish laughed.

"I think she looks rather formidable. You'd have to be, I suppose to leave the temperate climes of Spain for this remote corner of Scotland. Imagine what it must have been like for her, coming here to the Braemar estate?" he said, shaking his head.

"I think she was brave to dae so. And I suppose it means ye have a little Spanish blood in ye," Hannah replied.

"Tis' a fine portrait," Mr. McSween said, peering over Hannah's shoulder.

"Aye, and worth a pretty penny, too," Connor said, shaking his head.

"And this is what these devils wanted to get their hands on, is it?" Mr. McSween asked.

"Aye, the six portraits – worth a fortune," Hannah said.

The farmer shook his head

"And they'd burn down yer mother's croft for them. Tis' a wickedness, Hannah," he replied.

With the excitement of the chase now over, Hannah's thoughts returned to her mother and sisters. She wanted to return to the croft – what was left of it – and now she wondered what would become of them. They had no home, and no means of making a living, either.

"We should go back to my mother and sisters," Hannah said, and Hamish nodded.

"I'll come with you. Connor can go down to Balmoral and explain what's happened. These two can be taken into the care of the magistrate," Hamish said, glancing at Sir Geoffrey and his companion, both of whom remained silent.

"I'll stay and keep an eye on these two," Mr. McSween said, grinning at Hannah, who smiled back at him, knowing he would relish the task.

She, Hamish, and Connor set off across the moorland, choosing their path carefully until they arrived at bridleway leading to Mr. McSween's farm. The sun had risen now, and the early morning mist in the glen below was clearing to reveal the castle in all its glory.

They carried the paintings with them, and now they parted ways, Connor heading for Balmoral, and Hannah and Hamish returning to the croft.

They could see the rising smoke long before they came in sight of it, and it broke Hannah's heart to see her mother, sisters, aunt, and uncle, sitting forlornly on the heathers next to the smoking pile of rubble.

"Did ye catch them?" Hannah's mother asked, looking up as Hannah and Hamish approached.

"Aye, Mother. It was Sir Geoffrey who started the fire. He and his horse sank into one of the quagmires. Mr. McSween has them tied up, and Connor's gone down to Balmoral to bring help," Hannah replied.

Her mother nodded, though she displayed little by way of emotion at the news. Hannah sat down next to her and put her arm around her.

"We've lost everythin' – all we held dear, Hannah. And all because of another wicked aristocrat," Hannah's mother exclaimed, as tears rolled down her cheeks.

"It's all right, Mother. It'll be all right," Hannah replied, even as she was uncertain it would be.

But now, Hamish stepped forward, holding out one of the paintings and smiling at Hannah's mother, who looked up at him in surprise.

"Mrs. McGinn, I hope you don't count me amongst those foolish aristocrats you speak of," he said, and Hannah's mother shook her head.

"Nay, Hamish, I daene. But… we've lost everythin' – I'm happy for ye, truly, I am, but look at what we're left with," she said, sighing as the tears rolled down her cheeks.

"But I can help you. You didn't think I was going to take my fortune and leave, did you?" he asked.

Hannah's mother looked up at him in surprise. She wiped the tears from her eyes with the sleeves of her dress, as Hannah slipped her hand into her mother's and squeezed it.

"I… I daenae know. We cannae expect ye to help us," she said, but Hamish smiled.

"I'll rebuild the croft for you, and I'll make sure you never have to work another day in your life," he said.

Hannah smiled at him. He had proved the sincerity of his words, and now she could only be thankful for all he had done for them.

THE CROFTER'S DAUGHTER

"But… dae ye really mean it? Ye would rebuild the croft? Ye would help us?" Hannah's mother exclaimed.

"I give you my word, I will," Hamish replied.

The others, too, stared at one another in astonishment, even as Hamish now turned to Hannah's uncle, who shaking his head in disbelief.

"We owe ye a debt of gratitude, sir. If my brother was here, he'd say the same," Hannah's uncle said.

"And I'll see to it you have your operation – in Edinburgh or London. It can take place as soon as the arrangements can be made. I'll pay for everything," Hamish said, as Hannah's aunt gasped.

There was much rejoicing amongst the party, as now they laid out the six paintings on the heather, each of them representing a happy future for them all.

But as they looked at them, astonished at the good fortune which was now theirs, the sounds of horses hooves came from the moorland path, and looking up, Hannah could see half a dozen horses approaching.

"Goodness, what's this?" she exclaimed, as Hamish rose to stand next to her.

To her surprise, he gasped, turning to Hannah in astonishment.

"It's Prince Albert," he said, as the riders came into view.

BY ROYAL APPOINTMENT

*H*annah was amazed. She had never seen either the Prince Consort or the Queen, and now the rest of her family scrambled to their feet as the horses rode up to the ruins of the croft, and Prince Albert surveyed the scene.

"Dreadful... wicked," he exclaimed, dismounting his horse, and coming towards them.

Hannah was surprised to see her mother sink into a curtsey, prompted, it seemed, by Maeve and Caitlin, who had sunk so low they were almost sitting back on the ground.

Hannah and her aunt did the same, and the two men – Hamish and Hannah's uncle, who was supporting himself with a crutch – bowed.

"Yer Royal Highness," Hannah's mother said, as Hamish now stepped forward.

"It's very good of you to come, sir," he said, and Prince Albert shook his head.

"I'm sorry for all that's happened – your godmother's most concerned about the situation. She asked me to come at once. We had our suspicions over Sir Geoffrey, but this matter proves his lies and deceptions absolutely. To burn down a poor family's croft for his own gain – it's despicable, and… ah, are these the paintings?" the Prince Consort asked.

"That's right, sir. Aren't they magnificent?" Hamish said, and Prince Albert stooped down to examine them.

"Quite remarkable. I've read the account of them. And to think of the number of times we visited your uncle at the Braemar estate and didn't give them a second glance. Extraordinary. To see them first hand, I can hardly believe it," he said, shaking his head.

Hannah could not quite believe she was not dreaming. Here she was, standing in the presence of Prince Albert himself. He had come to see her and her family, and now he was discussing the paintings she had kept hidden for all these years in the roof space above the croft.

"And we've got Hannah and her family to thank for keeping them safe, sir. They've hidden them here in the croft ever since my uncle left them to me. I think he knew their value, even if it he couldn't prove it," Hamish said, and Prince Albert nodded.

"I'm sorry for all that's happened to you, Hamish – to you all. Your godmother and I… well, we shouldn't have allowed Sir Geoffrey to extend his influence over you. It was wrong. We didn't realise, you see," he said, shaking his head sadly.

"I don't hold it against you, sir. But I need your help now. I want to sell the paintings and recoup my fortune. Sir Geoffrey would've taken them for himself, but they're mine. He forged my uncle's will, I'm certain of it. I don't believe we're even related. He's a fraudster and a charlatan," Hamish exclaimed, clenching his fists with anger.

Prince Albert picked up one of the paintings, examining it and shaking his head.

"Remarkable… I want to acquire them for the royal collection. I know their worth, and I'll ensure I pay a fair price for them. Enough for you to re-establish yourself, Hamish, and live the sort of life a duke should live," he said.

Hamish stared at Prince Albert in disbelief, and Hannah gasped.

"I… I don't know what to say, sir," Hamish replied, and the Prince Consort laughed.

"Say yes, and what's more, I'll see to it this croft is rebuilt, and this family is rewarded for their efforts. How are you, Brendan?" Prince Albert said, turning to Hannah's uncle, who stared at him in astonishment.

"I… you know my name, sir?" he asked, and Prince Albert nodded.

"I pay you a pension, don't I? I'm concerned for all my estate workers. I was sorry to hear of your accident, and I was only too glad to grant you a pension," he said.

Hannah's uncle had tears in his eyes, and he thanked the Prince Consort profusely.

"I still need an operation, your Royal Highness, but it's thanks to your kindness I'm still here," he said, and Prince Albert smiled.

"There'll be plenty of money from the sale of the paintings to fund your operation. I'm sure Hamish can look after you, can't you Hamish?" he said, and Hamish nodded.

"I can, sir. I assure you," Hamish said, glancing around at the others, as Hannah still could not believe her good fortune.

Prince Albert now turned his attentions to the croft. The walls were gone, the roof burned up, and all the family's possessions burned.

They had nothing but the clothes they stood up in, and Prince Albert now directed the men he had brought with him to help the ladies and Hannah's uncle.

"I think breakfast at Balmoral, don't you? Then we'll find you some quarters. There's a delightful cottage on the grounds. You can stay there whilst we see about rebuilding your croft," Prince Albert said.

Hannah's mother turned to her in utter disbelief.

"I daenae know what to say, Hannah. They've saved us," she said.

Hannah knew her mother would be feeling conflicted. She had always made her feelings towards the Royal Family clear, and yet here was Prince Albert doing all he could to help them.

"Then they're nae so bad, are they, Mother?" Hannah whispered.

Their few meagre possessions were packed into a saddlebag, and now the party made its way along the moorland path and down through the woods towards the castle, led by Prince Albert.

"I can hardly believe it, Hannah," Hamish said, as the two of them walked side by side.

"Tis' remarkable. But will ye really stay? I'd understand if ye wanted to go back to London. Yer the Duke of Braemar, and I'm only a..." she began, but Hamish interrupted her.

"You're only my dearest friend, the person whose proved her loyalty to me these long years past, the woman who safeguarded the inheritance I now enjoy. Don't ever say you're nothing, Hannah, because you mean everything to me," he replied.

Hannah blushed as he slipped his hand into hers. She smiled at him, and they walked on together, following the party towards the castle, where they came on a remarkable scene.

A carriage – fixed with metal bars at the windows – stood outside the doors of the castle, and into it was being ushered Sir Geoffrey and his companion. They were both still covered in mud, their hands bound, and their heads bowed.

Mr. McSween was standing watching, and an official-looking man was supervising the procedure, assisted by two royal constables.

"The magistrate?" Hannah whispered, and Hamish nodded.

"Ah, excellent, that's them gone," Prince Albert said, as the carriage drew away.

"What's goin' to happen to them?" Hannah asked, forgetting for a moment she was addressing the spouse of the monarch.

"They'll be sent to the prison hulks, I hope. They won't trouble any of us again," Prince Albert replied, as now he ushered them into the castle.

Hannah remembered taking tea there, but her mother gazed around her in awe at the opulence of their surroundings.

"We shouldnae be here," Maeve whispered, but Prince Albert turned to her and smiled.

"Today, Maeve, you can be above stairs, not below. And I'm sure Hamish can see to it you remain permanently so," he said.

Maeve stared at him in amazement, and Hamish smiled.

"I certainly can," Hamish said, and Maeve shook her head in disbelief.

Prince Albert led them through into a large room, decorated in a baronial style, where a table was laid for breakfast, and a sideboard groaned under the weight of a lavish breakfast.

"Won't you all sit down? I've some business to attend to now, but eat your fill, and I'll make arrangements for the cottage. Hamish can look after you," Prince Albert said, and nodding to them, he left the room.

Hannah's mother let out a sigh, shaking her head in astonishment.

"I cannae believe what's just happened, and to think… we're sittin' in a dinin' room at Balmoral. Tis' a dream," she said, gazing around her at the room, where portraits gazed down from the walls and suits of armour stood to attention on either side of the fireplace.

The door opened and several footmen entered, accompanied by the butler, Wigmore, who bowed to them as the footmen began to pour cups of coffee and bring dishes from the sideboard. Together, they made a merry breakfast, and Hannah could not believe the good fortune which was theirs.

When breakfast was finished, the family were taken to their new lodgings – a cottage on the Balmoral estate where everything was provided for them. Hannah and Hamish lingered outside, whilst Hannah's mother and the others let out cries of exclamation from inside.

It was a handsome, whitewashed cottage, built in a clearing, and surrounded by a small garden, where all manner of beautiful flowers and vegetables grew.

"I hope you like it," Hamish said, and Hannah nodded.

"I like it very much, but I still cannae believe we're here. After all that's happened," she said, shaking her head.

"You deserve that happiness, Hannah. All of you do," Hamish said, taking Hannah by the hand and smiling at her.

Hannah's heart skipped a beat, and she blushed under his gaze, feeling grateful to him for all he had done.

"And ye dae, too. Ye've faced yer own tragedies. We both have. But we're stronger for them," she said, and Hamish nodded.

"But we don't need to face them anymore, Hannah. You don't have to live the life of a crofter anymore. Not now I've got my inheritance," he said.

Hannah looked at him in confusion. She did not understand entirely what he was saying.

"But… we still need to make a livin' – my family, I mean. I'll still have to work in the croft, when it's rebuilt," she said, but Hamish shook his head.

"Not if you're the Duchess of Braemar, you won't," he replied.

Hannah gasped, staring at him in astonishment. Did he really mean what he was saying?

"I… are ye askin' me to marry ye?" she stammered, and now he sank to one knee, still holding her by the hand, and gazing up into her eyes with a look of complete and utter love in his eyes.

"Yes, Hannah, that's just what I'm asking of you. I've thought about it ever since… well, the day I left Balmoral with that wicked devil now clapped in irons. I've thought of you every day, Hannah. I love you with all my heart. I couldn't imagine my life without you. I don't want to imagine my life without you. I know you'll find all manner of reasons to refuse me, but I beg you not to. Don't think of me as the Duke of Braemar, or a distant aristocrat. Just think of me as Hamish – the foolish boy who ran across the moorlands with you and couldn't stay still long enough to watch the stag," he said.

Hannah laughed. He was trying to convince her, but she needed no convincing. She loved him, and the thought of marrying him filled her heart with joy. At that moment, Sheppey appeared around the side of the cottage, and he barked, leaping into Hamish's arms, and licking his face. Hamish fell backwards, laughing as the dog nuzzled into him.

"Oh, Sheppey, ye silly dog," Hannah said, catching Sheppey by the scruff and pulling him back.

Hamish sat up, grinning, even as he had a nervous look in his eyes. Hannah smiled at him and held out her hand. He took it and rose to his feet, whilst Sheppey danced around their ankles.

"Well, Hannah – will you marry me?" he asked, and Hannah nodded.

"Aye, I will. With all my heart I say aye," she said, and Hamish breathed a deep sigh of relief and put his arms around her.

"Oh, Hannah. You don't know how happy you've made me. I've never been so happy in all my life. I thought… I thought I'd lost you. When I went away, I didn't know if… well, if you'd wait for me. I thought you'd find someone else. I didn't expect you to write to me each day, and that fleeting visit I made when I came to Balmoral for the reading of the will… when I saw you then, I fell ever more in love with you. But I was penniless. I had nothing to give you. I couldn't expect you to marry me without a penny to my name," he said.

He gazed into her eyes with a smile on his face, and Hannah gazed back, knowing she had found every happiness she had ever desired.

He kissed her, their lips lingering together for a moment before Sheppey barked questioningly. As their lips parted,

Hannah glanced down at the dog, who seemed confused as to what was happening.

"Have ye never seen two people in love, Sheppey?" she asked, and Hamish laughed.

"I don't think he has. He's looking at us very strangely. Come now, Sheppey – don't you know a duke and duchess when you see them?" he asked.

"I think he's still confused," Hannah replied, ad Hamish now reached into his pocket and brought out a small box.

"I couldn't get a ring, but I think you might recognise this," he said, and opening it, he revealed the butterfly Hannah had given him all those years ago, still perfectly preserved.

She smiled, taking the box, as a tear rolled down her cheek.

"I knew ye'd keep it safe," she whispered.

At that moment, the door of the cottage opened, and Hannah's mother, her two sisters, Connor, and Hannah's aunt and uncle emerged. Hannah and Hamish turned to them, and her mother looked at them in surprise.

"Did ye nae want to see the cottage, Hannah? Tis' a palace. I've never seen such a place – well, Balmoral, itself, but to think we'll be livin' there," she said, shaking her head in amazement.

"We'll come and see it, Mother, but… Hamish and I have somethin' to tell ye," Hannah said, glancing up at Hamish, who smiled.

"With your mother's permission, of course," he said.

"My permission for what?" Hannah's mother replied.

"For us to be married, Mother," Hannah replied.

Her mother's eyes grew wide, and she clapped her hands together in delight, staring at them both as a smile broke over her face. The others exchanged looks of delight, and Caitlin and Maeve both let out a shriek of excitement.

"Oh, Hannah, how wonderful," Maeve exclaimed.

Hannah was still looking at her mother, who now took a step

forward. There were tears in her eyes, and she held out her hands to Hannah, who now went to embrace her.

"My darlin' daughter. Tis' all I've ever wanted for you – to be happy. Nothin' more. I'm so sorry for ye've endured these long years past. Losin' yer dear father, and the hardships of our lives on the moor. But if yer father was here now, he'd be so proud of ye. Strong, determined, faithful – that's my Hannah. And I can think of nay one better than yer dear Hamish to be yer husband," she said.

Tears welled up in Hannah's eyes, and she threw her arms around her mother and kissed her.

"Thank ye, Mother. I love ye so much," she said, and her mother embraced her.

"I love ye, too. With all my heart, Hannah. Or should that be, yer grace," she said, and Hannah laughed.

"I'm nae a duchess yet, Mother," she said, as the others now offered their congratulations.

News of the happy betrothal soon spread, and later that day, a message arrived from the Queen herself, wishing the couple every blessing in their lives together.

"She writes I'm to have an audience with her later today – alone," Hamish said, reading through the note, which had been delivered by the Queen's equerry.

"What can she want to see ye about?" Hannah asked, as the two of them sat by the river that afternoon.

"I don't know, but I'd better go and get ready. I can't appear in front of Her Majesty in this dirty state. I'm still covered in mud from the quagmire," Hamish replied, and he went off to change and get ready.

Hannah sat a while longer, watching the waters flow by. Footsteps behind caused her to turn, and she looked up to find her mother coming towards her. She smiled at her, and her mother sat down next to her and put her arm around her, resting her head on Hannah's shoulder.

"I never thought I'd say this, but I'm glad the Royal Family came to Balmoral," she said, and Hannah smiled.

"I am, too," she replied.

Her mother turned to her and kissed her on the cheek.

"I'm proud of ye, Hannah. And yer father would've been proud of ye, too. I was wrong about ye and Hamish. I thought it was a fleetin' moment in the past. Yer first love. I saw how much it hurt ye to lose him, and I wondered why ye kept that flame alive in yer heart. I had so many doubts, but ye proved me wrong, the both of ye. I know he'll take good care of ye, Hannah," her mother said, and Hannah smiled.

"I know he will, too, Mother," she replied.

They sat for a while in silence amidst the peace and tranquillity of the Balmoral gardens, watching the waters of the river flow by. Birds were singing in the trees above, and a sweet floral scent hung in the air – the roses and lavender which grew abundance all around them. Despite everything that had happened, Hannah felt at peace, and she could only be grateful to Hamish for all he had done for her, and her family.

The Royal Family were not to blame for the troubles of the past, and she was glad her mother had come to realise that. At length, Hamish returned from his audience with the Queen, and Hannah's mother left them alone together, as Hamish sat down, shaking his head in amazement.

"I can't believe it, Hannah. It's remarkable," he said, taking her by the hand.

She looked at him in surprise, wondering what the Queen had said to make him appear so astonished.

"What's happened? What did Her Majesty say?" she asked, and Hamish smiled at her.

"She's gifted the home of the late Lord Leith to the Braemar estate. It's a magnificent house, a few miles to the west of Ballater, not far from here. There's a house and grounds, along with a section of the river, and a grouse moor, too. She's given me it as a gift for my marriage, and as a recompense for the things I've suffered these years gone by. She told me how sorry she was for what's happened and promised to do anything she could to help us in the future," he said.

Hannah was amazed by these words. She could hardly take them in. She had lived her whole life in a croft on the moor, and now she was to be mistress in a grand house and given the title of duchess.

It was astonishing, and she shook her head in amazement, hardly able to comprehend the changes lying ahead.

"Tis' a most generous offer," she said, and Hamish nodded.

"*The* most generous. We'll move there as soon as we're married. All of us – your family, too. We can rebuild the croft, of course, but your mother won't ever have to work again," he said.

Hannah smiled. She could only imagine what the rest of her family would say when they heard the news. Her uncle was to receive his operation. Maeve and Caitlin would no longer work as maids, and Connor would not have to work in the stables.

Her aunt and mother could leave behind their lives of hard work and enjoy all the comforts which wealth would afford them. The paintings had brought hope to them all, and it was all thanks to Hamish.

"Ye've done so much for us all," Hannah said, but Hamish shook his head.

"I never forgot the day my uncle died. I felt so alone, and yet I wasn't alone at all. I had you, your mother, and the rest of your family, too. You showed me what it was to have a family, Hannah. It sounds foolish, but it was the bread and dripping which proved it. It seemed to represent your mother's kindness, and yours, too. You'll call me a fool, I know, but it's how I feel."

But Hannah was not about to call him a fool. She knew how important family could be. To lose her family would be the greatest tragedy, and she could only imagine the pain Hamish had known at losing his parents, and then his uncle, too.

She took both his hands in hers and rested her forehead against his.

"Yer nae a fool. I know just how ye feel. We've both found what we were searchin' for. Fate brought us together and pulled us apart. But we were meant to be together, Hamish. I always knew we were, and now we are – forever," she replied.

He kissed her and smiled, running his thumbs along the edge of her fingers.

"I love you, Hannah," he whispered, bringing his lips to hers.

"And I love ye, too," she replied, and in that moment, it seemed as though time stood still, and all that mattered was the two of them together, sitting by river in the gardens of Balmoral, filled with hope for all that was to come.

THE HAPPIEST OF DAYS

"There now, tis' the last pin, Hannah," her mother said, stepping back to admire her handiwork.

Hannah looked at herself in the mirror, catching her sister's eyes, as Caitlin threaded a needle with white cotton.

"It will nae take me long," Caitlin said, smiling at Hannah, who stood rigidly still whilst her sister sewed in the alterations to the dress.

It was the day of Hannah's marriage to Hamish, and the cottage was a hive of activity and preparation.

Caitlin had come from the big house early that morning to assist. She was now second only to Her Majesty's own dresser, and she soon had the alterations made, stitching the dress with an expert eye.

Maeve, too, had helped Hannah to get ready, combing her hair, whilst Hannah's mother fussed with a set of jewels gifted the Queen herself for the occasion.

"Look at these pearls. I've never seen anythin' like them," Hannah's mother said, shaking her head.

"They came from India, apparently. Her Majesty was very gracious to gift them to me. Tis' a shame she and the Prince

Consort had to return to London before the weddin'—I was hopin' they would be there," Hannah said, as her mother placed the pearls around her neck.

"We have much to be thankful to them for," she said, stepping back to admire the jewels.

Caitlin now rose to her feet, nodding, as Hannah twirled the dress back and forth, admiring her appearance in the mirror. She still not could not believe that she—the daughter of a highland crofter—was marrying the Duke of Braemar.

And yet here she was, in a cottage on the grounds of the Balmoral estate, wearing pearls gifted her by the Queen herself, about to walk down the aisle and marry Her Majesty's godson. It felt like a dream, and yet it was very real.

Hannah had never felt so happy, and now a knock came at the bedroom door, and Caitlin went to answer it.

"Come in, Professor, tis' almost time," she said, ushering Professor Lochray into the room.

The professor was wearing a tweed suit and had a sprig of heather in his buttonhole. He beamed at Hannah and came to kiss her on the cheek.

"Ye look beautiful, lass. Tis' a great honour to be asked to give ye away. Yer father would've been the proudest of men," he said, and Hannah smiled.

"Thank ye, Professor. I couldnae think of anyone I'd rather have given me away than ye," she said.

The clock on the mantelpiece was approaching eleven O'clock, and they were due at the church for half past the hour. Caitlin made a few last-minute adjustments to the dress, and the party now left the cottage, walking the short distance through the gardens to the forecourt at the front of the castle, where an open carriage was waiting for them.

Connor was dressed in the outfit of a gillie—tweeds and breeches, and he, too, wore a sprig of heather in his buttonhole. Hannah's uncle and aunt were already sitting in the carriage,

CATHARINE DOBBS

and Connor helped Hannah up into her seat, followed by the others.

"Are ye ready?" he asked, and Hannah nodded.

"Aye, I'm ready," she said, even as her stomach was filled with butterflies, nervous with anticipation of what was to come.

They set off on the short drive to Crathie kirk, crossing the river over the bridge built by Prince Albert and designed by Isambard Kingdom Brunel. It was late summer, and the trees provided a welcome shade from the heat of the sun in the bright blue sky above.

Connor led the horses, and it was not long before they arrived at the gates of the church where many of the castle's servants, along with crofters from the moorland, had gathered to witness the occasion.

"Look at all these people, Hannah," her mother whispered as Connor helped them down from the carriage.

Hannah's uncle was walking with a crutch, and several people came forward to help him. Amongst them, Mr. McSween, who smiled at Hannah and doffed his hat.

"Ye look a bonnie lass," he said, and Hannah smiled.

"Tis' a bonnie day. Mr. McSween. And ye were there when it all began," she said.

"And so was I," a woman's voice replied, and Hannah looked up to the governess–Mimi–coming forward to greet her.

She stared at her in delight, knowing what Hamish would say when he saw her. She was primly dressed in a blue gown, with a shawl and bonnet, and it looked as though she had only recently arrived, still carrying an overnight bag in her hand.

"Mimi, how wonderful to see ye. Does Hamish know yer here?" Hannah exclaimed, and the former governess shook her head.

"No, he doesn't. I saw the announcement in the periodicals, and I knew I had to be here. I couldn't stay away. I loved Hamish as a boy. We went through so much together, and to think of him marrying you, Hannah… it's just wonderful," she said, and she embraced Hannah, kissing her on both cheeks as Reverend Macreedy came to greet them.

"Tis' a happy day, Hannah. A happy day, indeed," he said, and Hannah smiled.

"Is Hamish here yet?" she asked, and the minister nodded.

"Aye, he's inside, pacin' up and down. We shouldnae keep him waitin' any longer," he said, and now the professor offered Hannah his arm.

"Shall we, lass?" he said, and Hannah nodded.

She took a deep breath, glancing around at the others, all of whom were smiling at her. Her nerves were mixed with excitement at the prospect of what was to come. She was to marry Hamish, the man she had loved since first she had known him, the man she had not dared believe she *would* ever marry, and the man she would now spend the rest of life with.

How happy she felt at the prospect, and as she followed the minister into the church, it seemed as though her whole life had been building to this moment.

"God bless ye, Hannah, my darlin' daughter," her mother whispered, and now Hannah caught sight of Hamish for the first time.

He was dressed in a kilt and tartan, with a sporran hanging at his waist, and long pale coloured socks turned up at the knees. His waistcoat was green, and he, too, wore a sprig of heather in the buttonhole of the frock coat he wore over it. He looked very handsome and smiled at Hannah as she and the professor approached.

"You look beautiful, Hannah," he said, as the minster came to stand before them.

He cleared his throat, opening his prayer book to begin.

"Tis' a joy to welcome the two of ye to this kirk, where ye shall make yer vows before God and yer witnesses," he began, before reading a verse of scripture and beginning the marriage ceremony.

Hannah and Hamish exchanged simple vows, promising to love and cherish one another all the days of their life. They promised faithfulness in times plenty and times of hardship, and Hamish gave Hannah a ring, a symbol of their union. After the final blessing, the minister invited them to share a kiss, and pronounced them to be man and wife.

"Thank you, Hannah," Hamish whispered, as their lips parted.

"There's nothin' ye need to thank me for, Hamish. I love ye with all my heart, and I know ye love me, too," she whispered in reply.

"I do love you with all my heart, Hannah. The vows we made today… they mean everything to me, and I promise to uphold them for the rest of our lives together," he replied.

They turned to face the congregation, and Hannah could see her mother and sisters weeping into their handkerchiefs. Hamish now noticed Mimi at the back of the church, sitting alone on the last pew, and his face broke into a look of the utmost surprise.

"Dae ye see her, Hamish?" Hannah said, and Hamish nodded.

"Mimi, I thought… I thought I'd never see her again," he exclaimed, and now they hurried forward as his former governess came to greet them.

"I couldn't stay away from your wedding, could I, Hamish?" she said, embracing him and kissing him on both cheeks.

"I didn't know where you were, Mimi. I'd have invited you if I did. I'm so sorry we lost touch. That wicked man forbade me from having anything to do with my former life. I couldn't write to you," Hamish exclaimed, and Mimi smiled and shook her head.

"It doesn't matter now, Hamish. All that matters is you're happy. When I read about your engagement, I couldn't have been more delighted. I knew I had to come," she said as Hamish shook his head.

"I'm surrounded by the most wonderful people–all my

friends," he said, turning to Hannah, who put her arms around him and kissed him.

"And we've got all our lives to look forward to, Hamish," she said, as others now came to congratulate them.

It was a sizable party that left the church that day, returning to Balmoral to celebrate the happiness of the occasion with tea and cake in an opulently decorated salon, where a long table groaned with all manner of delights, and the guests mingled with one another long into the afternoon.

"Wasn't it wonderful?" Hamish said as he and Hannah stepped out onto the castle terrace and looked out across the river.

"I couldn't imagine anything more wonderful," she replied, and turning to her, he kissed her, the two of them now united in a bond that could never be broken, the bond of true love.

EPILOGUE

CATCHING A FISH

One year later

The salmon were jumping in the foaming waters of the river below, and Hamish helped Hannah down the bank onto a large rock, below which the river gushed. Spray was creating rainbows over the water, and Hannah smiled at the sight of the leaping fish, whose silvery scales caught the sunlight, sparkling as though they were covered in diamonds.

"There's so many of them," she exclaimed, as Hamish took a set of rods from the gillie who had accompanied them down from the bank.

"It's the season now, the river's filled with them, all dancing in the flood," Hamish said, nodding to the gillie, who now climbed back up the bank, leaving the two of them alone.

It had been Hamish's idea to come and fish at Balmoral. They had made the short journey along the glen by carriage from their home just west of Ballater. It was a year since their marriage, and they had settled well at the estate.

It was a beautiful house, and Hannah was proud to be its mistress. She had taken well to her knew life as Duchess of Brae-

THE CROFTER'S DAUGHTER

mar, and the Queen had appointed her as a lady in-waiting during her times of residency at Balmoral. Hannah had been terribly nervous to be in the Queen's presence, but the monarch had put her at ease, and introduced her as "my dear highlander's daughter, the Duchess of Braemar."

"I could watch them all day. The way they leap – tis' like the gillie's ball at the castle. They dance," Hannah exclaimed, watching as the fish sprang from the water.

Hamish was threading the rods, and he cast off, holding one for Hannah, who took it, watching as the line disappeared into the water.

"Have you got a tug yet?" Hamish asked, as she reeled it in.

"Tis' only my first try," she replied, laughing as he cast off his own rod and pulled it in without success.

Hannah was with child. The doctor had confirmed it a month ago, and she and Hamish could not have been more excited about the prospect of welcoming a child into the world.

The whole family were delighted, and Hamish had asked Prince Albert to be the godfather. He had accepted, and with the baby due in December, it seemed they would be celebrating Christmas with a new arrival.

"I haven't got a bite yet, either," Hamish said, casting off again.

Hannah did so, too, aiming her line at a deeper part of the river, where the water swirled before cascading into the foaming rapids below.

"Perhaps here," Hannah said, and Hamish shook his head.

"No, you won't get anything there, you..." he began, but before he could finish, the line went taut, and Hannah had to hold it tight as an enormous salmon emerged from water's depths, its glistening scales reflecting the sunlight.

"Look, Hamish, tis' magnificent," she exclaimed, as Hamish helped her to reel it in.

The fish was a giant, at least twice as big as any of the others they had seen jumping in the stream below, and Hamish waded a little into the water to bring it in.

"Remarkable, Hannah, quite remarkable. You should be jolly proud of yourself. Make sure you tell my godmother about this," Hamish said, holding up the fish, which had now stopped floundering.

Hannah smiled. She thought of her father. It had been on this part of the river where he died, and her own catch seemed symbolic of a memory laid to rest.

"It's for my father," she said, and Hamish nodded.

"I understand, Hannah," he said, setting down the fish and coming to stand next to her.

He put his arm around her, and she rested her head on his shoulder, glad to be alone with him, as now he placed his hand on her stomach.

"Dae ye think it will be a boy or a girl?" she asked, looking up at him.

He shrugged and smiled.

"I don't mind – it doesn't matter to me. If it's a girl, she'll surely have her mother's pluck and determination, her courageous spirit, and her kindness," he replied.

"And if it's a boy?" Hannah said.

"Then he'll have whatever qualities you think his father possesses. But I think there'll be a little of us both in the child, I hope so," he said.

At that moment, a bark came from the bank above, and Sheppey appeared, dragging the gillie on his lead.

"I'm sorry, yer grace, he wouldnae sit still. He kept whinin' for ye," the gillie called out, and Hannah and Hamish both laughed.

"Let him come down. He's sensible enough not to jump into the river," Hamish called out, and the gillie removed the lead, and Sheppey came bounding towards them, barking furiously.

"What would we dae without Sheppey? He'll have a surprise

when the little one comes along," Hannah said, and Hamish smiled.

"I think he'll be the loyalist of companions to the child, and I know you'll be the most wonderful of mothers," he replied, putting his arm around her, and kissing her, as Hannah rested her head on his chest, imagining all the happiness they had to look forward to as they spent the rest of their lives together.

If you enjoyed this story, could I please ask you to leave a review on Amazon?

Thank you so much.

Printed in Great Britain
by Amazon